THE SISTERS GRIMM

6

THE S
GRI

10th Anniversary Edition

6

STERS MM

TALES FROM THE HOOD

MICHAEL BUCKLEY

Pictures by PETER FERGUSON

AMULET BOOKS   NEW YORK

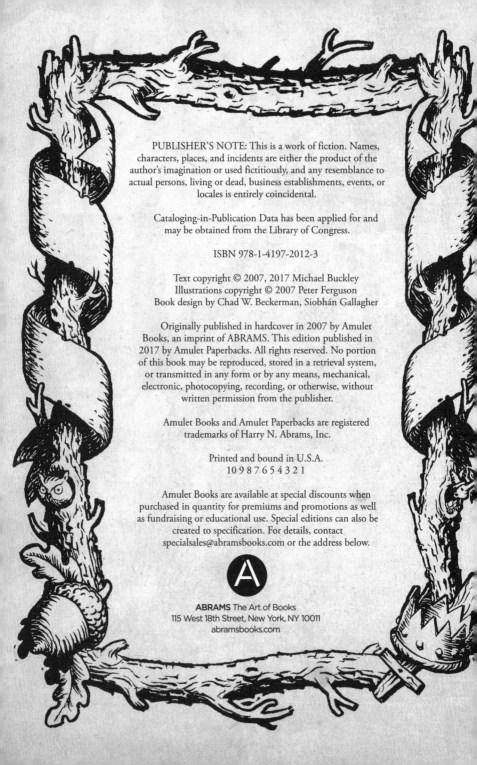

Cataloging-in-Publication Data has been applied for and may be obtained from the Library of Congress.

ISBN 978-1-4197-2012-3

Text copyright © 2007, 2017 Michael Buckley
Illustrations copyright © 2007 Peter Ferguson
Book design by Chad W. Beckerman, Siobhán Gallagher

Printed and bound in U.S.A.
10 9 8 7 6 5 4 3 2 1

Amulet Books are available at special discounts when purchased in quantity for premiums and promotions as well as fundraising or educational use. Special editions can also be created to specification. For details, contact specialsales@abramsbooks.com or the address below.

ABRAMS The Art of Books
115 West 18th Street, New York, NY 10011
abramsbooks.com

For my friend Joe Deasy

Sabrina had never before felt as confident as she did at that moment. For the first time in her life, she wasn't afraid of monsters or villains. In fact, she was eager for a confrontation. Let one of the Scarlet Hand's thugs try something—she would crush them into dust!

She wanted to tell Daphne how she felt. If only she could make her sister understand. But the words were too hard to find. Her thoughts were cloudy and confused. It didn't help that everyone was shouting and the wind was blasting in her ears.

Sabrina turned to her sister. A swirling black fog circled Daphne's body, blocking out most of the little girl's face. All Sabrina could see were her eyes, like two brilliant suns shining through the darkness.

"You have to fight this!" Daphne cried from behind the fog. "I know you are still in there. Don't let him control you!"

"Fight him, child," a voice said. Sabrina looked down to find Mr. Canis lying at her feet—his body, old and withered, pinned to the floor by a huge, fur-covered paw. It was squeezing the life from the old man's chest.

Sabrina cried out for help. Suddenly, she realized the paw that was killing Mr. Canis was her own.

1

Five Days Earlier

W HAT A CRAZY DREAM," SABRINA MUMBLED when she woke. In it, she had been walking along a stone path until she suddenly realized she was naked. She screamed and rushed to the bushes to hide. How could she have left the house without getting dressed? It was mortifying, but things only got worse. A moment later, Puck appeared. Since she had little alternative, she begged him to bring her a set of clothes. Much to her disbelief, he flew off and swiftly returned with a pair of jeans, a shirt, and sneakers. Then, he walked away so she could dress in private, leaving without so much as a snicker or a sarcastic comment. Relieved, she dressed quickly and continued on her way, only to find people staring and pointing as she passed them. She looked down to find she was completely naked again! She cried out for Puck, hoping he'd fetch her another set of clothing, but the boy fairy just shook his head in disappointment.

"Clothes can't hide who you really are, Sabrina," he said.

Even in her dreams, Puck was a pain.

Now she was awake and, thankfully, dressed in her pajamas. A cool breeze drifted through her bedroom window, causing the model airplanes hanging from the ceiling to sway back and forth. She watched them for a while, imagining her father building them when he was her age. He must have put a lot of effort into the models. They were beautiful.

Sabrina checked her alarm clock: 3:00 a.m. Now was a good time, she decided. There were no emergencies to deal with, no impending chaos, and—best of all—no prying eyes. Her little sister, Daphne, was still asleep, snoring softly into her pillow. She wouldn't wake until morning. Yes, now was the best time.

Sabrina slipped out of bed, knelt down, and reached under the bed to a loose floorboard. From beneath it, she retrieved a little black bag. She then tiptoed to the bathroom.

Once there, she closed the door and flipped on the light. Getting the room to herself for more than a few seconds was a special treat. There were a lot of people living in the big old house. In addition to the sisters, there were Uncle Jake, Granny Relda, Puck—and of course Elvis, the family dog, who often used the toilet as a drinking fountain. They all shared one tiny bathroom, and privacy was in short supply.

Sabrina spilled the bag's contents into the sink. It was a small but treasured collection of makeup she quietly bought whenever the family went into town: tubes of lip gloss, eye shadow, mascara, blush, and foundation.

"All right, here goes nothing," she whispered.

First, she smeared on the foundation, but it made her look like a ghost. To balance it out, she put on blush. Then she applied mascara, which was thick and gloppy, and she poked herself in the eye with the eyeliner pencil. After smudging some lipstick on, she took a step back to peer at herself fully the mirror.

Sabrina nearly cried. She looked like the joker from a stack of playing cards. She was hideous. How was she supposed to learn how to use this stuff?

She needed her mother. Veronica would know how to do makeup. She would explain all the things Sabrina was feeling but didn't understand, like why Sabrina's appearance was becoming more and more important to her. It seemed like just yesterday when she couldn't have cared less about how she looked, but now? It felt as if all she could think about was how others might see her. She hated herself for it.

Luckily, no one in her family had noticed her new preoccupation—most important, Puck. If he discovered she was visiting the bathroom in the middle of the night to primp, he would never stop making fun of her.

Sabrina scrubbed the makeup off her face and was about to go back to bed when she heard something bubbling in the toilet. The lid was down, so she couldn't see what was causing the noise, but she had her suspicions. Before Puck had moved into the house with the Grimms, he'd lived in the woods. Modern conveniences mesmerized him—none more so than the toilet. He loved to flush it over and over and watch the water swirl around and disappear.

For months, he was convinced toilets were some kind of magic, until Uncle Jake explained how plumbing worked. The newfound knowledge only increased Puck's fascination, and it wasn't long before he was conducting "scientific research" to discover what could—and couldn't—be flushed down the tubes. It started out with a little loose change, but the items quickly grew in size: marbles, wristwatches, doorknobs, balls of yarn, even—once—scoops of butter pecan ice cream. Granny finally put an end to the fun when she caught him trying to flush a beaver he'd found in the woods. Ever since, the toilet regularly coughed up Puck's "experiments." Last week Sabrina had found one of her mittens floating in the bowl. Now, apparently, something else was making its way to the surface. She hoped it wasn't the missing TV remote.

But when Sabrina lifted the lid, she found something so shocking, she would likely fear toilets for the rest of her life. A little man was sitting in the bowl.

"Who goes there?" he demanded in a squeaky voice. He was less than a foot tall and wore a tiny green suit, a matching bowler hat, and shiny black shoes with brass buckles. His long red beard dipped into the water.

Sabrina shrieked and slammed the toilet lid on the creature's head. He groaned and shouted a few angry curses, but Sabrina didn't stick around to hear them. She ran down the hallway, screaming for her grandmother.

Granny Relda stumbled out of her room wearing an ankle-length nightgown and a sleeping cap. She looked the picture of the sweet, gentle grandmother, except for the sharpened battle-ax she held in her hand.

"*Liebling!*" she cried in a light German accent. "What is all this racket?"

"There's something in the toilet!" Sabrina yelled.

Uncle Jake came out of a room at the end of the hall. He was fully dressed in jeans, leather boots, and his new overcoat covered with hundreds of little pockets he had sewn himself. He looked exhausted and in dire need of a shave.

"What's all the hubbub?"

"Sabrina saw something in the toilet," Granny Relda explained.

"I swear I flushed," Uncle Jake said as he threw up his hands.

"Not that!" Sabrina shrieked. "It was a person. He spoke to me."

"Mom, you've really got to cut back on all the spicy food you've been feeding the girls," Uncle Jake said. "It's giving them bad dreams."

"It wasn't a dream!" Sabrina insisted. "Come see for yourself."

Daphne entered the hallway, dragging her blanket behind her. "Can't a person get some shut-eye around here?" she grumbled.

"Sabrina had a bad dream," Granny Relda explained.

"It wasn't a dream!" Sabrina repeated. "There's something in the toilet."

"I swear I flushed," Daphne said.

"Ugh! I'll show you," Sabrina said, pulling her family into the bathroom. She pointed at the toilet. "It's in there!"

Granny set her battle-ax on the floor and smiled. "Honestly, Sabrina, I think you're a little old to be scared of the bogeyman."

The old woman lifted the lid. Inside was the little man, rubbing the top of his head and glaring angrily at the crowd.

"What's the big idea?" he growled.

The Grimms all cried out in fright. Startled, Granny slammed the lid down, and everyone backed out into the hall.

"Now do you believe me?" Sabrina asked.

"Oh my!" Granny exclaimed. "I'll never doubt you again!"

"What should we do, Mom?" Uncle Jake asked the old woman.

"Elvis!" Granny Relda shouted.

Seconds later, an enormous Great Dane barreled up the stairs, knocking a few pictures off the wall as he bolted to the bathroom. He barked at the toilet fiercely, snarling and snapping at the lid.

"Get him, boy!" Daphne ordered.

"You better surrender!" Uncle Jake shouted at the toilet. "Our dog is very hungry!"

Just then, another door opened down the hall, and a shaggy-haired boy in cloud-print pajamas stepped into the hallway. He scratched his armpit and belched. "Is there a war going on out here? Some people are trying to sleep!"

"There's something in the toilet!" Daphne shouted.

"Yeah, I probably forgot to flush," Puck said as he turned back to his room. "Enjoy!"

"Not that! There's a little man in it," Granny Relda said.

"Oh, you mean Seamus," Puck said matter-of-factly. "He's part of your new security detail."

"Security detail?" Sabrina repeated.

"Yeah. Now that Mr. Canis is in jail, you people need body-guards, and to be honest, I'm too busy to do it all myself. So I hired a team of experts."

"Why is he in the toilet?" Uncle Jake pressed.

"He's guarding it. Duh. The toilet is a vulnerable entrance into this house," Puck explained. "Anything could crawl up the pipes and take a bite of your—"

"We get the idea," Granny Relda interrupted. "What are we supposed to do when we need to use it?"

"Seamus takes regular breaks and has lunch every day at noon," Puck said.

"This is ridiculous," Sabrina said. "We don't need bodyguards, and we definitely don't need you to put some weirdo in the toilet!"

Seamus lifted the lid and crawled out of the toilet with an angry look in his eyes. "Who are you calling a weirdo? I'm a leprechaun. Puck, I didn't sign on for this abuse. I quit!"

"Quit? You can't quit," Puck insisted. "Who will I get to replace you?"

"Go find a toilet elf. What do I care?" the leprechaun shouted as he stomped down the hall, leaving a trail of little wet footprints behind him.

Puck frowned. "Now look what you've done. Do you know how hard it is to find someone to sit in a toilet all day and night?"

"How many more leprechauns are in the house?" Daphne asked, peeking behind the shower curtain.

"That was the only one," Puck said.

"Good!" Sabrina said, relieved.

"But there are a dozen trolls, some goblins, a few elves and brownies, and a chupacabra."

Sabrina gasped. "There are weirdos all over the house?"

"*Weirdo* is a really ugly term. This is the twenty-first century, you know," Puck replied. "Wait a minute. What's that on your lips?"

Horrified, Sabrina wiped her mouth on her sleeve, leaving a

lipstick stain on her shirt. She silently cursed herself for not washing thoroughly enough.

"Puck, we appreciate your looking after us," Granny said. "With Mr. Canis temporarily in the town jail, I guess it can't hurt to have a security detail around the house, but the bathroom might be the one place we don't need an extra set of eyes."

"Suit yourself, but if a dragon crawls up the pipes and toasts your rear end, don't come crying to me," Puck said, stomping off to his room.

Daphne peered into the toilet. "Could a dragon really fit in there?"

Granny Relda assured the little girl that she was safe from dragon attacks and encouraged everyone to go back to bed. "We're going to visit Mr. Canis bright and early tomorrow," she reminded them.

Another wasted trip, Sabrina thought to herself. The family had gone to see their old friend every day since his arrest. Every time, they'd been turned away by the sheriff.

Granny returned to her room, with Elvis trotting behind her.

"Hey, before you two go back to sleep, do you want to see where she is?" Uncle Jake asked.

"Absolutely," Daphne replied.

The girls followed their uncle to a room at the end of the hall. It was sparsely furnished, with only a full-length mirror against the far wall and a queen-size bed in the middle. Lying on the bed were Henry and Veronica Grimm, Sabrina and Daphne's parents, the victims of a spell that kept them sound asleep. Nothing Sabrina and her family had tried could wake them. But recently, the Grimms had found a glimmer of hope—they'd learned a woman from their father's past could break the spell. Unfortunately, this woman wasn't in Ferryport Landing, but the family had found a way to locate her.

The trio turned to the mirror hanging on the wall. This was no ordinary mirror: Instead of their reflection, a huge head with thick features floated in the glass, surrounded by black clouds and streaks of lightning.

"Mirror, we'd like to take a look at Goldilocks," Jake said.

"Jake, you know how this works. Poetry activates the magic," Mirror replied.

Daphne stepped forward. "Mirror, Mirror, my greatest wish is to know where Goldilocks is."

Mirror frowned.

"What?" Daphne said. "It rhymes!"

"Hardly! *Is* and *wish* do not rhyme."

"It's close enough!"

"Where is the rhythm? And the meter—atrocious!"

"Listen, if you want real poetry, read some Maya Angelou," Uncle Jake said. "Just show us Goldilocks."

Mirror frowned but did as he was told. Gazing into the silvery surface, Sabrina saw a beautiful, curly-haired woman appear. She had a round face and green eyes. Her button nose was painted with a splash of freckles, and her blond hair looked like sunshine. She wore a billowy white dress and was perched atop a camel. There were other people with her, each on their own camel. Everyone was snapping pictures of an ancient pyramid rising out of a rocky desert.

"Goldilocks," Sabrina whispered.

"Wherever she is, it looks hot," Daphne said, peering into the mirror.

"I think it's Egypt. The place is overrun with pyramids," Uncle Jake said.

"Last week she was in the Serengeti, the week before—South Africa," Daphne said.

Uncle Jake shrugged. "She's only ever in one place for a few days, and then she jets off somewhere completely different."

"How are we going to get a message to her?" Sabrina growled. "She has to come back here. She has to help us wake up Mom and Dad!"

Daphne and Uncle Jake seemed taken aback by Sabrina's sudden temper, but she had a right to be angry. Their mission to break the sleeping spell had once felt hopeless. Now they had a solution, and it was almost harder than before. Watching Goldilocks dart around the world on her silly vacations and not being able to speak to her was maddening.

"Be patient, 'Brina," Uncle Jake said soothingly. "We'll track her down."

Mirror's fierce face appeared in the silver surface.

"Is there anything else I can help you with, folks?" Mirror asked.

"Not unless you can drag Goldilocks away from Egypt and bring her here," Jake said.

"I'm afraid that's not one of my abilities. Speaking of dragging, though—girls, could you drag your uncle out of here? He's been lurking in front of me for two weeks. He needs something to eat and, if you ask me, a long-overdue bath."

"Mirror!" Uncle Jake cried.

Daphne sniffed the air. "You are a little rank."

Uncle Jake sighed and threw his hands up in surrender. "Fine! I get it! You two should run off to bed. You heard your grandmother: You've got another big day tomorrow of sitting outside the jail, hoping to see Mr. Canis."

"You're not coming with us?" Daphne asked her uncle.

"Not this time, peanut. I've got plans."

"Briar Rose plans?" Sabrina asked.

"Holding hands and smooching plans?" Daphne asked.

"If I play my cards right." Uncle Jake winked. "Girls, I have to confess. I think the princess is the one."

Daphne's face cracked into a wide grin. "I call dibs on being the flower girl at the wedding."

"Let's not get too far ahead of ourselves," Uncle Jake said, but he was grinning just as widely.

Granny Relda's cooking left a lot to be desired. Many of her signature dishes included strange roots, rare flowers, milk from unusual animals, and tree bark, all in heavy, bubbling sauces. But that morning, Sabrina's appetite was ruined not by her grandmother's cooking, but by a small, pig-snouted creature sitting on the table. It had beady red eyes, large blisters all over its face, and a long, blue, forked tail it used to swat the flies that circled its melon-shaped head.

"I suppose you're part of the security team," Sabrina said to the creature, which nodded and puffed up its chest proudly.

"I'm a poison sniffer, I am. My job is to sniff out anything that might kill ya before you put it in your gob, if it pleases you, miss."

"My gob?"

"Your piehole, your chowder box, your mouth," it said as it wiped its runny nose on its extremely hairy arm. "I'm to take a snort of every bite. Puck's orders."

"So, we're all just going to accept this madness?" Sabrina asked the empty room. Uncle Jake was already gone for the day, Daphne was doing something secretive in the bathroom, and Puck rarely woke up in time for breakfast.

Granny rushed into the room carrying a sizzling pan. She flipped something that looked like a pink burrito onto Sabrina's plate.

"What is this?" Sabrina asked as she poked at it with her fork. She worried that it might squeal.

"It's porcupine bacon in a rosebush-grub wrap with heavy whipping cream," Granny said as she rushed back to the kitchen.

Sabrina handed her plate to the ugly creature. "I'll give you five bucks if you tell my grandmother this is poisoned."

The creature shook its head. "I cannot be bought, I say."

Granny returned with a pitcher and poured some glowing red juice into Sabrina's glass.

"Your sister has something planned for all of us," the old woman announced, gesturing at Daphne's empty chair. "She told me that today she is going to be a totally different person."

"A person who eats with a fork?" Sabrina asked.

"Don't tease her. She's gotten it into her head that she needs to grow up. When she comes down, try to treat her like an adult," Granny said.

Sabrina cocked an eyebrow. "You're kidding me, right?"

Just then, Daphne stepped into the room, and Sabrina nearly fell out of her chair. Gone were her sister's goofy T-shirts, the denim overalls, the mismatched socks. Daphne was wearing one of Sabrina's nicest dresses. Her hair was combed straight rather than braided in her usual pigtails, and she was wearing lip gloss. She sat in her chair, placed her napkin in her lap, and smiled. "I hope everyone slept well."

It was several moments before Sabrina realized her jaw was hanging open. "Is this some kind of joke?" she asked bitterly. Clearly, Daphne had found her makeup bag and was mocking her.

Daphne frowned, as did Granny Relda.

"No, it's not a joke," Daphne snapped, then did something that made Sabrina's blood boil. She turned to their grandmother and rolled her eyes impatiently. *How dare she?*

"So, I hear we have some appointments this morning, Grandmother," Daphne said.

Granny chuckled under her breath. "Yes indeed. I need the two of you to hurry with breakfast. We're going downtown."

"How?" Daphne asked. "Uncle Jacob took the car for his date with Briar."

"And if you think we're getting into Rip van Winkle's cab again, you've lost your mind." Sabrina shuddered, recalling their last hair-raising ride with the narcoleptic taxi driver.

"Oh, no. We'll be taking the flying carpet," Granny explained.

"Shotgun!" Daphne cried, then cleared her throat. "What I meant to say is that it sounds quite pleasant."

It was Sabrina's turn to roll her eyes.

After breakfast, Sabrina, Daphne, Granny Relda, and the

strange, food-smelling creature (who insisted on coming along as protection) sailed over Ferryport Landing aboard Aladdin's flying carpet. It was just one of a number of magical items the family owned, and one of Sabrina's least favorite. Her first ride on the enchanted rug had nearly gotten her killed, as it seemed to have a mind of its own. But, thankfully, it obeyed Granny's every command.

Along the way, Sabrina gazed down at the town. Everything was changing. The once-quaint neighborhoods were now completely abandoned. Many homes had been demolished, and, in their place, odd, sinister-looking buildings had been erected—castles surrounded by alligator-infested moats and mansions made from ice. Even Mr. Applebee's farm, the site of their first detective case, was being converted into a gigantic chessboard reminiscent of the one in Lewis Carroll's *Through the Looking-Glass*. The morphing landscape made Sabrina uncomfortable. It was a stark reminder that the Scarlet Hand was taking over Ferryport Landing and that the Grimms were the only humans left.

"There's Main Street!" Daphne shouted over the wind, and seconds later the carpet gently touched down outside the Ferryport Landing National Bank. Once everyone had stepped onto the sidewalk, the rug neatly rolled itself up, and Daphne hoisted it onto her shoulder.

"Wait here and stay out of sight," the pig-snouted creature said.

"I'll scout the neighborhood. There could be bandits and archers in the trees."

"I'm sure there are no—" Granny started, but the little monster raced off before she could finish.

"Well, I can't say I'm too unhappy to be rid of him," Granny said. "He claimed everything I made for breakfast was toxic."

"He wasn't wrong," Sabrina mumbled to herself.

Granny led the girls down the street. It was a particularly lonely day downtown. The sidewalks were empty and the roadways deserted. The town's one and only traffic light was burned out. As far as Sabrina knew, Ferryport Landing had never been a boomtown, but the little stores that lined Main Street had always been filled with customers. Now, they stood abandoned. Signs hung in windows declaring emergency liquidations. One read, AFTER 200 YEARS IN BUSINESS WE'RE CLOSING OUR DOORS. Another sign—an ominous red handprint, the mark of the Scarlet Hand—hung in many windows. Sabrina spotted one nailed to the door of Old King Cole's restaurant.

"We're running out of places to eat in this town," Daphne grumbled. Normally, Daphne's single-minded obsession with eating would have made Sabrina smile, but the little girl made a troubling point. The town was closing its doors to humans and any Everafters who didn't join the Scarlet Hand.

Eventually Granny stopped outside of a small office building with huge picture windows and a manicured lawn.

"What are we doing here?" Sabrina asked. "I thought we were going to the jail."

"We've been going to the jail every day for a month, and we haven't been allowed to see Mr. Canis. I don't think that's going to change, so I've decided to hire someone who can help."

Daphne looked up at the building. "We're going to meet an Everafter, aren't we?" The little girl loved meeting fairy-tale characters. She squealed with delight and bit her palm whenever she was in the presence of one. Sabrina was sure meeting a new one would force her sister to give up this new, sophisticated version of herself.

"I guess it won't be such a big deal now that you're a grown-up," Sabrina teased.

"No big deal at all," Daphne said seriously.

Their piglike security guard raced around the corner, breathing heavily and shooting them all panicked looks.

"You should have stayed put!" he said through wheezes. "This place ain't safe, I say."

"Well, luckily we have you," Granny said sarcastically.

The group went inside the building and climbed the stairs to the third floor. There, they found a door that read THE SHERWOOD GROUP: ATTORNEYS-AT-LAW, SUING THE RICH AND GIVING TO THE POOR SINCE 1887. Sabrina scanned her memory for the name Sherwood, but nothing came to mind.

Granny opened the door, and they found themselves in the middle of a chaotic battle. A number of men in business suits were sword fighting, arm wrestling, and drinking beer from tall ceramic mugs, all singing a rambling English fight song at the top of their lungs. Once one song was finished, the men broke into another.

"Hello?" Granny Relda called out, but the men didn't seem to notice her. They kept playing their violent games, laughing, and dancing.

"I should get you out of here," the bodyguard squeaked. "These men are barbarians."

"We'll be fine," Granny assured the creature. "I'm told that this is how they behave all the time. We're perfectly safe."

Just then, a potted fern flew past them and smashed against a wall. There was a loud cheer that suddenly died when the men noticed the family had nearly been hit.

"Gentlemen! We have clients," a huge man with a dark, un-tamed beard shouted. He stood more than six and a half feet tall and had a chest as wide as a car. His hands were each as big as basketballs. He had a fierce, wild expression on his face that was offset by his beaming smile. "Welcome to the Sherwood Group!"

"Welcome!" the men shouted in unison as they held up their beers.

"I have an appointment with Mr. Robin Hood," Granny said.

Sabrina glanced at her sister, waiting for the little girl to squeal or bounce with happiness, but Daphne caught her looking.

"No big deal, huh?" Sabrina asked.

Daphne shook her head, though it was obvious she was struggling to hold in her excitement.

One of the sword-fighting men sheathed his weapon and rushed to greet Granny. He was tall and handsome, wearing a dark green pinstriped suit and sporting a red goatee and moustache. His wavy hair hung to his shoulders, framing a broad smile and bushy eyebrows that gave him a mischievous appearance.

He kissed Granny's hand. "Welcome, Mrs. Grimm. I'm Robin, and these are my merry men. Who do you want to take to court?"

2

ROBIN HOOD AND HIS BURLY COMPANIONS LED the family to an office lined with floor-to-ceiling windows with an amazing view of the Hudson River. The sun was creeping over the mountains, and its rays painted the waves a glittery gold. A tiny sailboat floated by, and a few hungry seagulls drifted over the water in search of breakfast. The Sherwood Group offices were tastefully decorated. Bookshelves filled with thick legal books lined the walls. A large mahogany desk sat in the center of the room. The only things that seemed out of place were a bow and a quiver of arrows mounted above the doorway.

The pig-snouted creature was not impressed. He scouted the room, peeking into a potted plant and beneath a leather sofa before crossing his arms and stationing himself near the exit.

"I apologize for the commotion when you arrived," Robin said. "You can take the men out of the forest, but you can't take the forest out of the men. May I introduce my associate, Little John?"

"Happy to meet you," the huge man roared. Sabrina reached out to shake his hand, but he swatted her on the back in what he must have thought was a friendly pat. It nearly knocked her to the floor.

"Mr. Hood, these are my granddaughters, Sabrina and Daphne, and our security guard."

"Security guard?" Little John said, eyeing the piglike pint-size creature.

"It's a dangerous town," the beast snarled.

"Indeed it is. Mrs. Grimm, I hope you'll call me Robin," he said as he bent to kiss her hand once more. "And I've heard quite a bit about the famous sisters Grimm." He patted Sabrina on the head like she was a beagle, then invited the family to have a seat.

"How can we be of service?" he continued.

"I need a lawyer," Granny Relda said.

"Then you've come to the right place," Robin said as he took a seat and put his feet up on his huge mahogany desk. "Were you injured on the job? A victim of malpractice? Bought some toys with too much lead paint?"

"No, nothing like that. Sheriff Nottingham arrested a friend of mine a month ago, and he has refused to let us visit him."

Robin and Little John shared a worried look.

"The Wolf," Little John said. The man's voice was filled with dread.

"We prefer to call him Mr. Canis," the old woman replied.

"Nottingham has not filed any charges against him. I can't imagine it's legal to hold someone this long without evidence of a crime."

Little John shook his head. "It's not, Mrs. Grimm, but I'm not sure we can help. First of all, the town has slipped into lawlessness since our new mayor was elected. Second, we're not criminal defense lawyers."

"He's right. We're litigators," Robin said. "We sue corporations that spill chemicals into rivers or make dangerous products. We help people win settlements when they slip on the sidewalk. We've never argued a criminal case."

"You must have some training," Granny said. "The only two criminal defense lawyers who lived in Ferryport Landing were human, and the mayor has run them out of town."

"Hiring me will only make your problems a million times worse," Robin said. "The Sheriff hates me even more than he hates you and your family."

"We're desperate."

Robin Hood got up from his desk and gazed at the river. Little John joined him, and the two men talked in low voices for several moments. They seemed to be having an argument, but eventually the men nodded and shook hands. Robin and Little John turned back to the family.

"Mayor Heart will shut this office down by sunset," Robin declared.

Granny sighed with defeat and stood up. Sabrina and Daphne did the same. "I understand. We won't waste any more of your time."

Suddenly, Robin Hood leaped forward to block the door. "I didn't say we wouldn't do it!"

"You'll take the case?"

"It's been a long time since I've been a thorn in Nottingham's side," Robin said with relish.

"We wouldn't pass this up for the world," Little John bellowed. "I'll get Friar Tuck started on the paperwork."

"Good thinking, my large friend," Robin said, then gave the family a wink. "As for us, we have an appointment with my favorite sheriff!"

Fifteen minutes later, Robin Hood pushed open the doors of the police station, followed by Sabrina, Daphne, Granny Relda, and Little John. The ugly little bodyguard, who Sabrina had learned was a miniature orc named Barto, was close behind. Sabrina found him painfully annoying, but Granny refused to send him home.

The police station was a mess. Boxes of files were scattered everywhere, many tipped over and rummaged through, then abandoned. There were huge maps of the town taped to the walls, all covered in scribbled writing. The front desk was stained with coffee-cup rings.

Robin rang the tarnished brass bell on the front counter. The chime was answered by an enraged growl from a back room.

"WHAT NOW?" a voice shouted.

"There he is," Robin said as his face broke into a mischievous smile.

"As pleasant as ever," Little John added.

A door flew open, rattling the full-length mirror that leaned nearby. Nottingham barreled into the room like an angry bull, his black cape flapping behind him. When he spotted the Grimms, he snarled—but when he saw Robin and Little John, he looked like his head might explode.

"You!" Nottingham roared as he pointed an angry finger at the lawyers.

"Us," Robin replied. It was obvious to Sabrina that these three men shared a long, bumpy history. She made a mental note to read up on Robin Hood's adventures when she got a chance.

Nottingham stood silently, studying the group the way a hyena watches its prey. The scar that started at the tip of one eye and ended at the corner of his mouth seemed to pulsate with every angry breath. Sabrina had seen the same expression on his face the night he tried to kill Daphne.

"Interesting outfit you've got there, Nottingham," Robin commented.

Aside from the cape, the sheriff was wearing leather pants and knee-high boots. His shirt was black and billowy, with silver buttons carved in the shape of human skulls. He had a sheathed dagger strapped to his waist.

"Is this what they mean when they say something's old-school?" Little John added. "You do realize this isn't the fifteenth century, right?"

"There's nothing old-fashioned about this," Nottingham said, brandishing his dagger.

"Oh, Nottingham, you've always enjoyed your dramatics," Robin said. "We didn't come here to fight you. We came to see our client."

"Client? What client?"

"Mr. Canis."

Suddenly, Sheriff Nottingham's rage was replaced by roars of laughter.

"I'm glad you're amused," Robin said. "I find what is passing as the rule of law in this town just as funny. You arrested Canis four weeks ago and have yet to charge him with a crime. If you aren't going to charge him, you must set him free—that's the law in Ferryport Landing."

"*I* AM THE LAW!" Nottingham shouted. "I'll do what I want with that monster. He's a murderer, and he'll hang for his crime, if I have anything to say about it."

"I remember a time when you used to say the same thing about me," Robin replied. "As for Canis—a murderer? Who was the victim?"

Nottingham chuckled. "Don't tell me you haven't heard the story? It goes a little something like this: A child wearing a red cloak journeyed to visit her poor, sick grandmother. A monster came along and ate the grandmother. No one lived happily ever after."

"That happened six hundred years ago!" Granny exclaimed.

"Justice has no time limit," the sheriff replied.

"Well, if justice is what you're after, then there must be a trial. I need to meet with Canis to prepare his defense," Robin said.

"Trial?" Nottingham scoffed. "You don't give a rabid dog a trial—you put him to sleep before he can hurt anyone else."

"You're going to kill him?" Sabrina asked, horrified.

Daphne burst into tears.

"Oh, here come the waterworks," the sheriff said, his face full of mocking concern. He bent over and took Daphne's chin in his gloved hand. "Save your tears, little one. You're going to need them."

Little John grabbed Nottingham by the arm, jerking him away from the girl. The sheriff wrenched himself free, and he and Little John glowered at each other.

"Let us see the old man before my friend here loses his temper," Robin warned.

"Never let it be said that I don't have a kind heart," Nottingham growled. "I'll let you all see your precious pet one last time before he goes off to doggy heaven."

The sheriff led the group down a long, filthy hallway to an iron door. He pushed it open with a creak. Inside was a large room split into four separate jail cells, two on either side with a walkway down the center. A lone fluorescent light dangled from the ceiling, blinking on and off.

"You've got visitors, mutt," Nottingham said, running his dagger along the bars of one of the cells. The high-pitched screech it made was deafening. "Have your chat and make it quick."

In the farthest corner a hulking figure was huddled against the wall. His limbs were bound by enormous chains. Sabrina felt a tingle in her belly that grew stronger and stronger as the family approached: It was clear the chains, the cell, and maybe even the entire jail were enchanted. Magic was the only way to keep the old man imprisoned. Normal chains could never hold a creature as strong as the Big Bad Wolf.

Sabrina smelled something rank: a combination of filth, sweat, and something less identifiable, something wild. It reminded her of a visit to the Bronx Zoo. While she'd watched the lions in their pit, a zookeeper tossed in slabs of raw meat for the animals. The lions fought over the scraps, roaring and snapping their jaws.

Granny approached the cell, unfazed. "Old friend," she said softly.

There was a rustling in the dark, and a deep voice broke the silence. "Go away, Relda."

"We've come to help you," Daphne said, joining her grandmother at the bars. "We hired lawyers. We're going to get you out of here."

Nottingham laughed again.

Robin took a small recording device out of his suit pocket and turned it on. "Mr. Canis, we're working to release you. I'm sure we can clear this up soon. In the meantime, you've been arrested for murder, and it would be in your best interest to tell me everything you remember about the crime."

"You're wasting your time," Canis said. "I have no memory of the event. I rarely know what the Wolf does."

"If you don't remember anything about the crime, then we can't be sure you're guilty," Little John said.

Canis shook his head. "I'm guilty."

"Mr. Canis, I don't think you understand, we—" Robin Hood began.

Canis leaped to his feet and let out a horrible roar. It was only then that Sabrina realized how much the old man had changed during his imprisonment. At his full height, Canis was nearly eight feet tall. His arms were so long that his ugly, clawed hands dragged on the ground. His ears, pointy and sprouting hair, were not on the sides of his face, but on the top of his head. His nose

and mouth had become a furry snout with glistening fangs, and his once-white hair was now brown flecked with black.

Sabrina's mind reeled. How could Canis have changed so much in four short weeks? She was sure this had to be a twisted joke, some kind of terrible prank cooked up by Nottingham for his own amusement. But then she saw the proof that this creature was her old friend: The beast was wearing a black patch over his left eye. It covered a wound Nottingham had inflicted not long ago. There was no denying it. This monster, this vicious Wolf, was breaking free of Mr. Canis's control. Out of instinct, Sabrina leaped forward and pulled her sister and grandmother to safety.

"Sabrina!" Granny cried, bewildered. There was disappointment and anger in her voice. "You have nothing to fear."

"Do not scold her, Relda," Mr. Canis said. "She may be the only one in your family who sees me for what I truly am. You'd be wise to pay more attention to her."

Granny shook her head, denying his words.

"What have you done to him?" Daphne demanded, lunging at the sheriff with her fists clenched. It took all of Sabrina's strength to hold her back.

"Control your brats, Mrs. Grimm, or they'll be enjoying the cell next to your hound," Nottingham said.

"Relda, I appreciate what you are trying to do for me, but nothing will help," Canis insisted. "Take the girls and leave. I don't need your lawyers. I'm right where I belong—in a cage. Fighting the Wolf for control over this body is a constant battle, one I am quickly losing. When I can no longer fight him, it is best if I am under lock and key."

"That's not going to happen," Daphne said. She reached through the bars and took Canis's huge hand in her own. A memory flashed in Sabrina's brain—once, not so long ago, the Wolf had grabbed Sabrina around the neck with that hand. The memory made her shiver down to her toes.

Sheriff Nottingham ran his dagger against the cell bars again. "Time's up!" he snarled. "Get out of my jail."

"We'll be back," Little John promised Mr. Canis.

Canis crawled back into the shadows, into the corner of his cell. "Do not waste your time on me," he murmured as they left.

That afternoon Robin Hood called to update Granny Relda. As he'd predicted, Mayor Heart and Sheriff Nottingham had come to the Sherwood Group offices with an order to seize the property and premises. The merry men were tossed out into the street. Robin and Little John were forced to continue their work from an empty table at Sacred Grounds, a coffee shop run by Uncle Jake's girlfriend, Briar Rose. Much to everyone's surprise, Robin and Little John were thrilled.

"I don't know if Briar's coffee shop can handle that crowd. The whole bunch of them sound rip-roaring drunk," Granny Relda said when she hung up the phone. "They're celebrating being Nottingham's biggest annoyance again."

"Being as merry as those guys are can't be good for their livers," Uncle Jake said.

Unfortunately, Robin had some more bad news: He and Little John were running into one roadblock after another in their efforts to free Mr. Canis. The town's government had collapsed since Mayor Heart's election. Nottingham hadn't made a single arrest other than Mr. Canis, and it seemed as if he and Heart were making up laws as they went along. Worse still, there was nothing the family could do to help with Canis's case. When Granny offered, Robin informed her that the best thing they could do was to stay by the phone and wait for updates.

The Grimms all tried to keep themselves distracted. Uncle Jake kept an eye on Goldilocks. Granny busied herself making earthworm crepes. Puck lay on the couch trying to break his personal record for most farts in an hour. Sabrina and Daphne turned their attention to the family's enormous book collection, researching everything they could find on the Big Bad Wolf.

The girls' father had kept fairy tales out of their house, leaving the sisters at a tremendous disadvantage now that they were knee-deep in the family business of investigating Everafter crimes.

"No one told me this story," Daphne said, pointing to the book she was reading, her face pale and frightened.

"Which story, *liebling*?" Granny Relda asked as she came in from the kitchen.

"The story of Little Red Riding Hood," she said, as she held up a copy of *Grimm's Fairy Tales*. "Jacob and Wilhelm called it 'Little Red Cap.' This version is . . . gross."

Puck leaped up and rushed across the room, suddenly interested. "Gross, how?"

"He eats Red's grandmother," Daphne said.

"That's awesome!" Puck exclaimed.

Sabrina ignored Puck. "I thought he killed her."

"Eating someone usually kills them," Puck said matter-of-factly.

"It says here that Red's mother sent her into the forest with a basket of food," Daphne explained. "She was supposed to take it to her sick grandmother, but along the way she met the Wolf."

"What kind of mother sends her kid into the woods alone? What did she think was going to happen?" Sabrina asked.

Daphne ignored her sister and continued. "Red made the mistake of telling the Wolf where she was going and he raced ahead, ate her grandmother, then put on her clothes."

"Creepy," Puck said admiringly.

"When Red showed up at the house, he ate her, too. But that

can't be right," Daphne commented, looking up from the book. "Little Red Riding Hood is alive."

"And crazy as ever," Sabrina said. Just thinking about the little girl gave her goose pimples. Luckily, Red had been admitted to the Ferryport Landing Memorial Hospital's mental-health ward. Just a few months prior, the little girl had stomped through town with her pet Jabberwocky, causing serious mayhem. She'd even tried to kidnap Granny Relda in a delusional effort to recreate her own lost family.

"We can't completely trust this story," Granny explained. "There are a lot of facts that don't add up, and there are many, many versions. The brothers didn't actually witness the crime, either. It happened hundreds of years before they wrote it down."

"My father told me the story once," Puck said. "There was a hunter or something—a woodsman who saved Red and her granny by cutting the Wolf's belly open and freeing them. Then he loaded the Wolf's belly up with stones and tossed him into the river to drown. I'd like to meet that guy. He's totally hard-core!"

"Who cares how many versions there are of the story? The Wolf eats people in all of them, doesn't he?" Sabrina asked as she glanced at the open pages of the heavy book. There was a gruesome illustration of the Wolf attacking the little girl.

Puck nodded. "He tried to kill the Three Little Pigs, too, and a whole family of talking lambs."

Uncle Jake and Granny shared a knowing look.

"Mr. Canis used to have some anger-management issues," Uncle Jake admitted.

Sabrina's mind was spinning with all the new information. "Did he really do all this?" she asked the old woman.

Granny lowered her eyes.

Sabrina was dumbfounded. "And you let him live here with us? You left us alone with him! He slept in a room right across the hall!"

"The Wolf is the murderer, Sabrina. Mr. Canis is not responsible," Granny said.

"Mr. Canis is the Wolf!" Sabrina insisted.

"No, Sabrina," Granny snapped. "Mr. Canis and the Wolf are two separate people. My friend would never hurt you."

"Your friend shares a body with a monster," Sabrina replied. "We've seen him tap into the Wolf's power. And he's been gradually transforming into the beast for months."

"OK, everyone, let's calm down," Uncle Jake said.

But Granny kept arguing. "Mr. Canis has always been in control, ever since the pigs got ahold of him. It wasn't until recently that he has struggled, but he will find the strength to fight again, and then everything will go back to normal."

"Mom, you saw him today," Uncle Jake said. "What are we going to do if he can't fight the Wolf?"

"Mr. Canis is right. The best place for him is behind bars. If the Wolf takes over, there will be no way to stop him," Sabrina cried.

"Mr. Canis is our friend!" Granny Relda shouted. Her face turned red, and her lips quivered in anger. Sabrina had never seen the old woman lose her temper so quickly or so fiercely. "Sabrina Grimm, go to your room!"

Sabrina reeled back. "What? I haven't been sent to my room since I was seven years old!"

"Then it's long overdue!"

"Mom, she hasn't said anything that isn't true," Uncle Jake said.

"Another word out of you, Jacob, and I'll send you to bed, too!"

Rattled, Sabrina marched up the steps and slammed her bedroom door. She threw herself on the bed and fought back tears. Crying would mean admitting that she was a child and that her opinions were easily dismissed. No! This time she was right. Granny could punish her all she wanted, but someone needed to speak up.

"Are you well?" a voice asked from under the bed.

Sabrina leaped up. "Who's there?"

"I'm part of your security detail," the voice said. "I'm guarding your bed."

"I could really use some privacy right now," she groaned.

"Sorry, boss's orders. I can't—"

"If you don't get out of here right now, I'm going to punt you through the window," Sabrina snapped.

A moment later, a little creature with a bright red nose, batlike ears, and furry feet crawled out from under the bed. He brushed a few dust bunnies off of his fur. "I suppose I could take a coffee break," he grumbled, then was gone.

Sabrina expected her grandmother to come apologize for losing her temper and to tell her that everything was going to be OK. But, after several hours, the old woman still had not appeared. Daphne and Uncle Jake were no-shows, as well. So was Puck, whom she expected to stop by, if only to gloat. Once, Elvis poked his head in. She called to him, but the big dog disappeared down the hallway. Even the family pet was against her.

She was hardly surprised. Sabrina never seemed to do or say anything right. She knew she was a constant source of disappointment to the others. She had been trying very hard to embrace her responsibilities, especially her detective training. She had resisted for months, but now she was actually enjoying some of it. She excelled in tracking criminals, finding clues, and self-defense. Just last week, Granny had praised her for her quick thinking and eye for detail.

How could her grandmother think Sabrina was so smart last week and, now, so wrong about Canis? He'd admitted to everyone that Sabrina was the only one in the family who saw him for what he was.

Around suppertime, there was a knock on the door. Someone left a tray with chicken baked in a gravy that smelled like pureed crayons and blueberries. She took a few bites, then pushed it away.

Later that evening, there was another knock. Daphne poked her head inside. "Is it safe to come in yet? The bed troll said you threatened to kick him out a window."

"It's safe. In fact, I'm glad you're here. We need to talk."

"Fine," Daphne said, crossing the room to the desk, then opening a drawer. She took out a string of pearls, tried them on, and then finally turned to Sabrina.

"Mr. Canis's not dangerous anymore. You know it, too. We've been here for months, and he's never hurt any of us."

"He's changing, Daphne."

"What should we do, then? Turn our backs on him? Let Nottingham and Heart kill him? That's what they're going to do, you know."

Sabrina couldn't argue with her sister. The mayor and the sheriff would kill Canis. She didn't think it was a bluff.

"We should get the weapon," Sabrina suggested.

Daphne reached into her shirt and pulled out a chain. Hanging from it was a small silver key. "Mr. Hamstead gave us this for emergencies only."

"This is an emergency," Sabrina argued. "If we're going to free

Canis, we need to be prepared. Let's face it, the guy is getting hairier and angrier by the day. You saw him freak out at the jail today. It's only going to get worse. It's best if we have the weapon, just in case. If he finds a way to get ahold of himself, then great—we'll just put it back in the safe-deposit box. Or, even better, we could use it to fight the Scarlet Hand. If whatever is in the box can control the Wolf, it can certainly take care of them. We might even be able to get rid of Puck's stupid security team."

"That would be nice. I found an elf munching on my socks in the hamper this morning," Daphne said.

"Then it's settled. Give me the key. I'll sneak out tonight and go get the weapon."

Daphne hesitated. "No. Whatever is in that box is magic, and you shouldn't use magic. It does bad things to you. Besides, Mr. Hamstead gave the key to me, so I get to decide when we use it."

Sabrina was furious. "Daphne, if this is part of your 'I'm a big girl now' routine, you need to cut it out. This is important!"

"I said no, and I mean no," Daphne snapped.

Sabrina was tempted to snatch the key right off Daphne's neck, but a knock at the door distracted her. Uncle Jake entered.

"How's it going?" he asked.

"Great! The whole family hates me!" Sabrina said sarcastically. "Is Granny still mad?"

"Let's just say the last time I saw her this angry, your father and I had used a magic wand to turn a teacher into a billy goat. Ms. Junger nearly ate her own desk by the time Mom found out and forced us to change her back."

Sabrina groaned.

"I tried to defend you, but listen, I don't even have a bedroom to be sent to. She might have made me sleep on the porch," Uncle Jake continued. "But, Sabrina, what did you expect? Mr. Canis is your grandmother's best friend. Did you really think she'd give up on him? Your father and I learned long ago that when it comes to the old man, you have to hold your tongue."

Sabrina's brow furrowed. "You've argued with Granny about him, too?"

"Sure. So did your grandfather," Uncle Jake replied. "When Canis showed up on our doorstep, my father refused to help him, but Mom has always seen the good in people. She invited him to live here, and it drove Dad nuts. He was sure Canis would change back and eat us all in the dead of night. Your father and I used to block our bedroom door with heavy furniture when we went to sleep. We kept baseball bats under our pillows. We all felt like you do now, Sabrina."

"If all of you felt like that, then how come I'm the bad guy now?" Sabrina asked.

"Because after all this time, after everything he has done for our family, you still won't give Canis the benefit of the doubt. He's proven his loyalty to us time and time again. He's saved all of our lives a million times over, and he has never allowed anyone to lay a hand on my mom. When the Jabberwocky killed my father, Canis dug the grave. I was destroyed. I blamed myself and didn't even stick around for his funeral. I decided to leave. I found Canis waiting for me on the edge of town. He begged me to stay, told me Mom needed me, but I wouldn't listen. He promised to watch over my family for me until I returned. Then he gave me a hug."

"No way!" Daphne cried in disbelief.

"It was the most uncomfortable hug of my life, but I knew I was leaving my family in good hands. I've never spoken badly about Canis since, and I never will again. I trust him with my life."

"But even he told us to leave him alone," Sabrina argued.

"He's giving up, but we can't. My mother never will, and that's why she's mad at you, kid. It breaks her heart that you can't see the goodness in others. Listen, I didn't come up here to give you a lecture," he said. "In fact, the warden has given me permission to release you, but I do have one last word of advice. If you want to know who a person truly is, you need to look. Now, if we're all done with our squabble, I could use your help."

"With what?" Daphne asked.

"I have an idea for how to communicate with Goldilocks," he said.

Suddenly, the argument was forgotten, and the girls dashed into the hallway, eager to help their uncle find the elusive Everafter. Mirror was waiting for them when they arrived.

"Mirror, show the girls what you just showed me," Uncle Jake said.

Goldilocks appeared in Mirror's surface. She was standing on the balcony of an elegant hotel. There were vines climbing along the walls and pretty boats floating on the water below. She looked radiant as the sunshine lit up her face.

"She sure is pretty," Daphne said.

Uncle Jake smiled. "Your dad has always had great taste in women, though I never understood what they saw in him."

Sabrina glanced over to her sleeping father. From what she had managed to piece together, he and Goldilocks had once been in love, years before he met Sabrina's mother. The tragedy that killed Grandpa Basil split them apart. Goldilocks was not at all how Sabrina had imagined her. She'd assumed the mysterious Everafter would resemble her own mother, Veronica, but they were complete opposites. Goldilocks wore fancy dresses, and her hair was never out of place. Sabrina's mom, who could easily have been a beauty queen herself, had an easy, casual style. She loved blue jeans, flip-flops, and baseball caps. Sabrina realized she was comparing the two women, and a twinge of betrayal stabbed at her heart. Goldilocks might be pretty, but she was no Veronica Grimm.

"After her trip to the pyramids, she headed to the airport and hopped on a flight," Uncle Jake said, filling the girls in. "I couldn't tell which one, but she seemed like she was in a hurry. She didn't even check any bags."

The image in the mirror dissolved and was replaced with a view of a flag fluttering in the breeze. It was bright red with a border of thorny vines, and at its center was a golden winged lion. The lion wore a halo and brandished a sword. Sabrina had never seen anything like the flag and wanted to study it further, but once again, the image changed. This time, she saw a mailbox labeled with the number 10 and stuffed with mail. Sabrina squinted at the letters, hoping an address might reveal itself, but what little she could make out was not written in English. Then the mailbox was gone, too, replaced with an elegant sign mounted on the side of a luxury hotel. It read HOTEL CIPRIANI.

Uncle Jake was smiling from ear to ear. "Cool, huh?"

"I'm confused," Sabrina said. "We've been watching her travel around for a month. What's different about this time?"

"The difference is, this time we have the name of her hotel!" Uncle Jake exclaimed. "All we have to do now is find out where this hotel is located, and we can contact her."

"I think that flag we saw might be a big clue," Sabrina said.

"I agree. If we can find the country it belongs to, we can narrow down our search. The language on the letters looked like Italian to me, but that doesn't necessarily mean she's in Italy. Italian is spoken all over the world. She could be in Slovenia or San Marino. Italian is even an official language of Switzerland."

"So how do we find out for sure?" Sabrina asked.

"The library, of course," Uncle Jake said.

Sabrina and Daphne groaned in unison. "Not the library."

"What's wrong with the library?" Uncle Jake asked.

"Nothing. The library is fine," Sabrina reassured him. "It's the librarian who's the problem."

"He's a complete idiot," Daphne explained.

Uncle Jake laughed. "There's no arguing that, but he's still the smartest guy in town. The two of you need to get over there right away. We have to find this hotel before Goldie flies off somewhere new."

"We're going to need the flying carpet to get to the library," Sabrina said.

"Then I need the key to its room," Mirror replied.

Sabrina reached into her pocket for her keys, but before she could hand them over, Puck charged into the room.

"Uh-uh-uh-uh-uh," he said. "You two aren't going anywhere without protection."

"Forget it! You're not sticking us with another one of your so-called bodyguards," Sabrina snapped.

"The last one was very gassy. Even gassier than you!" Daphne complained.

"Then put clothespins on your noses. Almost everyone in this town wants you dead. Not that I can blame them. But if you croak, the old lady will want to have a funeral, and if there's a funeral, she's going to make me take a bath. So I will superglue a hobgoblin to your back if you don't cooperate," Puck declared, then turned to Sabrina. "Do we have an understanding, dogface?"

Sabrina fumed. She was so angry she thought she might burst into flames. It wasn't Puck's stupid security team, it was his insult—dogface. It shouldn't have mattered to her—he insulted her all the time—but this one stung. Why did it suddenly matter to her that he thought she was ugly?

"What? No comeback?" Puck pressed, clearly surprised.

"Fine, then you have to be our bodyguard. You can fly us to the library," Daphne suggested.

"Excellent idea," Uncle Jake said.

"Bo-ring!" Puck yelled.

"Am I hearing you right, Puck? I was told you were a master of mischief. I guess you're too mature to sneak out without my mother knowing. These days you seem to act more like a good little boy than the so-called Trickster King. In fact, I'm surprised people don't mistake you for that other boy who won't grow up. What's his name?"

"Don't you say it!" Puck warned Uncle Jake.

"You know, the one who hangs out with the little girl and her brothers. He can fly, too," Daphne said.

"I mean it! Don't insult me by saying his name! That guy is a washed-up has-been!"

"Oh, I remember," Uncle Jake said, pretending to ignore the angry boy. "You're acting like Peter—"

Puck suddenly morphed into a lion. He let out an angry roar before returning to his true form.

"FINE!" he shouted. "I'll take you, but let's get one thing straight. I am not some silly flying boy in green tights. I am the Trickster King: the spiritual leader of hooligans, good-for-nothings, pranksters, and class clowns. I am a villain feared worldwide, and don't you forget it!"

"Of course you are," Uncle Jake said, giving the girls a wink.

Puck extended his wings, snatched the girls by their hands, and whisked them out the open window. Sabrina watched her uncle wave good-bye as the trio soared high over the forest.

3

THE MID-HUDSON PUBLIC LIBRARY WAS A SMALL building not far from the train station. Its parking lot was empty. When humans had lived in Ferryport Landing, the little library was a bustling community center. Now that they were gone, it was lonely and dark.

Sabrina's mother had loved to watch Westerns on television. Each film seemed to be set in the same barren, dusty ghost town. The library felt just as abandoned. Sabrina half expected tumbleweeds to roll by.

Puck sniffed the air and crinkled his nose.

"I smell books," he said, repulsed.

"That's probably because this is a library," Sabrina said, rolling her eyes. "It's full of books."

"Why didn't you warn me?" The boy looked absolutely horrified.

"What did you think a library was?" Daphne asked.

"I don't know," Puck replied. "I was hoping it was a place where men fought grizzly bears with their bare hands. I should have guessed. You two never do anything fun."

"Oh, you're not going to be bored in here. The librarian is sort of unpredictable. Stay alert, or you could get hurt," Daphne warned.

"We should have brought football helmets," Sabrina said.

"You two are teasing me," Puck complained.

"Fine! Don't believe us," Sabrina said. "You'll see soon enough."

Once inside, the trio found the library in a terrible state. Books, magazines, and newspapers lay scattered about the floor as if a cyclone had blown through the stacks. Overturned chairs were everywhere, but they didn't see a single living soul.

Puck perked up. "This looks promising."

"Let's just find what we're looking for and get out of here. If we're lucky, we won't have to see the librarian at all," Sabrina said.

Daphne started at one end of the stacks and Sabrina took the other, scanning the titles as they walked for a book on international flags.

"Look at all the learning. I'm going to be sick!" Puck cried, gagging.

"Can you give it a rest?" Sabrina snapped.

"And the smell! Books reek!" Puck groaned. "I can almost taste them."

"Stop being a baby," Daphne called from the next row over.

Her tone startled Sabrina. She had never heard the little girl scold anyone, especially Puck. Daphne usually thought everything he said or did was hilarious. Even more shocking was the expression on Daphne's face when they met at the end of the aisle. Daphne was impatiently rolling her eyes again. It was the rudest thing Sabrina had ever seen her sister do, and it made her furious. She was just about to lecture the little girl on manners when she heard someone whistling happily from across the room.

"He's coming," Daphne whispered.

"Is that the lunatic you were talking about?" Puck asked.

Sabrina clamped her hand over the boy's mouth. "Shut up! Maybe he won't find us," she whispered.

"Hello!" a voice sang out. The children spun to find the librarian standing right behind them. He seemed to be a tall, thin man. But his face was a burlap sack with eyes, a nose, and a smile painted in bright colors. Hay stuck out of his collar and sleeves, and a diploma wrapped in a red ribbon was stuffed in his breast pocket. He looked like any number of scarecrows that guarded the farms all over Ferryport Landing, except he was alive.

"You're a scarecrow," Puck said, uncharacteristically surprised. Puck's stories were always filled with weird creatures, but apparently a scarecrow librarian was something he had never seen before.

"Actually, I'm *the* Scarecrow: accomplished thinker, former Emperor of Oz, and head librarian of the Mid-Hudson Public Library."

Puck eyed the man closely. "But you're made out of hay, right?"

"Yes, and a brain. It was a gift from the great and terrible wizard."

"Someone gave you a brain?" Puck asked. "Whose was it before you got it?"

"I'm n-not sure what you mean," Scarecrow stammered.

"The brain! The wizard had to get it from somewhere. I bet it belonged to an arsonist. Those are the easiest to get," Puck rambled.

"My brain was brand-new!"

"If you say so, but it's much more likely that it is secondhand."

Scarecrow looked as if he might have a nervous breakdown.

Sabrina eyed the teetering stack of books in the librarian's arms. "Do you need any help?"

"Everything is under control," Scarecrow said, but that didn't seem to be true. The ceiling-scraping stack swayed back and forth, threatening to topple over at any moment. Sabrina shuffled the group to one side in hopes of avoiding the tower's dangerous lean, only to have to move again when it tilted back in their direction.

"I'm just hunky-dory! I suppose you are hot on the trail of another mystery."

The top book on the stack slipped off, but Scarecrow's leg darted out to catch it before it hit the floor. He stood balanced on one leg, as if he barely noticed his precarious position.

"We're actually looking for a book about flags," Daphne said.

"Excellent! Follow me!" Scarecrow hopped up and down on one leg toward the information desk. His hopping made the tower of books sway even more wildly, keeping Sabrina, Daphne, and Puck on the move to avoid the inevitable avalanche.

"He's definitely got a used brain," Puck whispered.

Just as the librarian reached the desk, a banana peel slipped out of his pocket and onto the floor. "OH! I'm losing my lunch!"

Sabrina groaned, knowing full well what was about to happen. She watched helplessly as Scarecrow slipped on the peel and went flailing, flinging the books into the air. Sabrina threw her hands up, but there was no escape from the painful shower of books.

Puck snatched his sword and used it to bat the books away. He brushed himself off frantically as if the books were poisonous spiders. "Get them off me!" he shouted.

"Clumsy me," the librarian cried, wobbling to his feet. He tried to help the children up but slipped on the peel once more, this time completely somersaulting in midair and landing flat on his back.

"Tell me about this flag of yours," he said, sitting up.

"It's red with a big golden lion with wings in the center," Daphne said. "There are vines on its border."

Scarecrow stood and rubbed his burlap chin in thought, then his eyes lit up. "I've seen that flag!" He raced off, and the trio chased him through the stacks, finally catching up with him in the back of the library. He clambered up a big bookcase, reaching for a book at the very top. The bookcase teetered back and forth under his weight.

"Does anyone else see where this is going?" Daphne sighed.

"I think I know why Dorothy wanted to go back to Kansas," Sabrina replied. She remembered seeing the movie *The Wizard of Oz* when she was little. Scarecrow was a lovable klutz, but the real flesh-and-hay version was almost intolerable. Then again, nearly everyone she met from Oz had a zany quality that got on her nerves. It didn't help that the same wizard who gave Scarecrow his brain had kidnapped her parents and tried to kill her.

Luckily, the shelf did not topple over, but that didn't mean the children were in the clear. Scarecrow pulled out every book and tossed down the ones he didn't need. The tumbling volumes were thick and heavy. Sabrina felt like she was trapped in a game of whack-a-mole.

"Ah! Here it is!" Scarecrow cried, just before he fell from the shelf and landed in a heap on the floor. Without missing a beat,

he sprang to his feet and opened the book. Inside were pictures of flags from all over the world. He flipped through the pages until he found the one the girls had seen hanging at the Hotel Cipriani.

"That's it!" Daphne said.

"That's the flag of a city called Venice," Scarecrow said proudly. "It's a lovely place, built on one hundred and seventeen islands connected by one hundred and fifty canals. In Venice, you don't hail a cab, you hail a boat called a gondola, because many of the roads are actually waterways. The population is roughly two hundred and sixty thousand people. The average annual rainfall is fifty inches. The major industry is tourism, and the region's biggest exports are textiles, glass, paper, motor vehicles, chemicals, minerals, and nonferrous metals."

Sabrina prepared for Daphne to ask for the definition of *nonferrous*; she herself had no idea what it meant. But much to Sabrina's surprise, the little girl took a pocket dictionary from her jacket and looked up the word on her own.

"*Nonferrous* describes a metal containing little or no iron," she announced.

Sabrina grabbed the dictionary. "What's this?"

"What does it look like?" Daphne said, rolling her eyes.

Sabrina could have screamed. How dare Daphne be so impatient with her?

"Anything else I can help you with?" Scarecrow asked.

Sabrina pushed down her anger and turned to the librarian. "You wouldn't be able to help us find an address in Venice, would you? We're interested in a place called the Hotel Cipriani."

"I'm on it!" Scarecrow raced back through the library to where the travel guides were kept, and once again the children were caught in a hailstorm of books as he climbed the stacks. Scarecrow finally snatched the one he wanted and held it triumphantly above his head. In his excitement, he lost his balance and nearly fell off the bookcase.

"Don't worry, kids. I've got everything under control," Scarecrow said, holding on with one hand and struggling to regain his footing. Suddenly, the entire bookcase tipped over and crashed down, burying Puck in a mountain of books.

"The books! They're touching me," he groaned.

Working together, the girls heaved the shelf off of Puck and Scarecrow. When the fairy boy got to his feet, he was covered in blotchy red marks and his face had swollen to the size of a pumpkin. He scratched his arms and legs furiously, then reached for the wooden sword he kept at his waist. Sabrina worried Puck was going to attack the clumsy Scarecrow, but instead he used the weapon to scratch his back.

"He actually is allergic," Daphne said.

Scarecrow grabbed a large volume off the floor. "Here it is!" He opened it and flipped through the pages. "This is a travel guide to Italy. It lists all the best hotels, restaurants, and places to sight-see. Oh, here—the Hotel Cipriani. It has a five-star rating—very swanky."

"Is there an address?" Sabrina asked.

"Absolutely! The listing says it's at Giudecca 10," Scarecrow said. "They put the building number after the street name in a lot of European countries. Is there anything else you need to know?"

"I'm not sure we'd survive any more of your help," Daphne grumbled. "Thanks a lot."

"Thanks are not necessary!" Scarecrow sang, ignoring Daphne's comment. "Learning something new is the best reward. Though I could use a hand reshelving these volumes."

Scarecrow strolled away, leaving the shelf and the books where they'd fallen. Puck stomped his feet and shouted after the librarian walked away, "I think that brain of yours has an expired warranty! I wouldn't be surprised if it was made out of an old sock and a pocketful of loose change! I hope the wizard kept the receipt!"

"Well, you can't say the library is boring anymore," Daphne said to him.

Puck scratched furiously. "I can still smell the books on my skin!"

Though Sabrina was eager to get home to tell Uncle Jake what they had learned, Daphne insisted they help with the mess. The girls reshelved all they could while Puck kept his distance from the stacks.

"Books are heavy," Daphne complained as she shelved a series of increasingly thick novels about a boy who went to a school for wizards.

"Excuse me," a voice said from behind them. Sabrina nearly screamed when she turned around. Standing before her was the strangest-looking man she had ever seen. He wore a white suit, and each of his fingers was adorned with a silver or ruby ring. On his wrist he wore a diamond-encrusted watch and, in each ear, a silver hoop earring. But most striking were his long curly beard and bushy eyebrows, both an unnatural shade of blue. Everything about him seemed inhuman, like he was the devil made flesh.

"Do you work here?" he asked.

Sabrina shook her head, speechless.

The blue-haired man frowned. "The fool who calls himself a librarian is nowhere to be found. I don't suppose you can point me to the law books?"

Sabrina shrugged. "Sorry."

"I'll find them myself." The man growled and walked deeper into the library.

Puck pulled the girls behind a shelf. "Do you know who that was?" he hissed.

The girls shook their heads.

"That was Bluebeard. He's only the most villainous Everafter in this town!"

"I thought you were the most villainous Everafter in this town," Sabrina challenged.

"Besides me," Puck said, peering around the corner to watch the blue-haired man.

"Maybe he'll give you an autograph," Sabrina snapped impatiently.

"Shhhh!" he whispered. "Bluebeard is a legend. He's famous for being married almost fifty times, and—in the end—each of his wives lost her head."

"You mean he drove them crazy?" Daphne asked.

"No, I mean he chopped their heads off with an ax, duh!" Puck snapped.

"Gross!" Daphne cried, craning to get a better look at the man.

"He stored his wives' bodies in a secret room in his home. Every time he remarried, he told his new wife to stay out of it. Of course, curiosity eventually got the best of them, and he kept adding to his collection."

Sabrina watched Bluebeard pulling several leather-bound books off a shelf. He sat with his stack at a nearby table and started flipping through them while taking notes on a big yellow pad.

"What do you think he's doing here?" Daphne asked.

"Evil stuff, duh!" Puck said.

"Let's go. He gives me the creeps," Sabrina said.

As they turned to leave, they were stopped in their tracks by a familiar face. Snow White entered the library with several books in her hands. She set them down on an empty table, sat, and started reading. Her arrival was not lost on Bluebeard. He stared at her for several long, uncomfortable moments. Sabrina had seen how men often reacted to the beautiful teacher. Snow was stunning, with coal-black hair and twinkling blue eyes, but Bluebeard's interest seemed darker than that of a man marveling at a pretty face. His gaze didn't fall on her so much as reach out for her, coaxing her to come closer. Sabrina was reminded of a film she'd seen in school about spiders catching flies in their webs, then eating them from the inside out. Bluebeard watched Ms. White the way a predator watches prey.

"Snow White?" Bluebeard called, standing up from his table and crossing to her.

Snow turned, and her ever-present smile disappeared. "Mr. Bluebeard."

"I haven't seen you in years. You're looking lovely," he said, flashing a mouth full of crooked teeth.

"Thank you," the teacher muttered. Sabrina could tell Ms. White was nervous: The beauty knocked one of her books off the table. Bluebeard swooped down to retrieve it, but he didn't give it back, ignoring Snow's outstretched hand.

"It's such a small town, but I never run into you like this," Bluebeard continued.

"Well, I keep quite busy."

"Oh, it's good to be busy. Keeps the mind from wandering," the man said. "You know what they say: 'Idle hands are the devil's playground.'"

Sabrina watched Snow force a smile and nod.

"Since we really don't get to see enough of each other," Bluebeard continued, "perhaps I can persuade you to accompany me to dinner. I'd love to 'catch up,' as they say."

Ms. White squirmed. "That's a very kind offer, but I just ended a relationship and I don't think I'm quite ready to date."

Bluebeard's eyes flashed with anger. "You're saying no to me?"

Snow stood up, knocking the rest of her books to the floor. Bluebeard shoved her back into her chair.

"I'm trying to be nice, Ms. White," he hissed.

"We have to stop this," Daphne declared.

"What do you want to do?" Sabrina asked.

Puck stepped in front of them. "Listen, this isn't a guy you play around with. If you go over there and get mixed up in Bluebeard's business, he'll make you regret it."

"She needs our help," Daphne insisted.

Sabrina glanced around, looking for a distraction. She spotted Scarecrow dangling from a bookcase halfway across the room. As before, the case was teetering back and forth. She had an idea.

"Help me push this bookcase over," Sabrina said. She pushed

on the frame, and it leaned a little. With Daphne and Puck's help, it was soon rocking back and forth, but it seemed like it might just as likely fall back on them.

"I think we need a little something extra," said Puck. He winked, spun around on his heels, and morphed into a bull with long white horns. With a grunt, Puck charged forward, headfirst, into the shelf. It toppled over, crashing into the bookshelf next to it, starting a chain reaction throughout the library. Like huge dominoes, they all fell one by one. Books and magazines crashed to the ground, as did the librarian, who was quickly buried beneath a pile of encyclopedias.

Sabrina knew Scarecrow was practically indestructible, so along with Puck and Daphne, she dashed toward the doors, chasing a fleeing Snow White. Once outside, Snow leaned against her car and patiently calmed her breathing. She was obviously unnerved by the encounter.

"Are you OK, Ms. White?" Daphne asked.

"Daphne?" Snow replied. "Yes, I just ran into . . . well . . . did you three just cause that mess?"

"Naturally." Puck grinned and bowed.

"We had to do something," Sabrina said. "We saw what Bluebeard was doing and thought you needed help."

"He's always had a thing . . ." Snow said with a shudder, as if even talking about Bluebeard frightened her. "Thanks for the assist."

"Ms. White, why haven't you returned any of Granny Relda's calls?" Daphne asked. "She wants to apologize."

Snow took a deep breath. "Daphne, when you grow up, you'll find that some things that seem simple are actually incredibly complicated, especially in matters of the heart."

"You mean love. Gross." Puck gagged.

"First of all, I am very grown up," Daphne said. "Second, Granny feels terrible about hiding Billy in our house, but he begged us to keep his secret. He's doing everything he can to try to protect you."

"Protect me from what?"

Sabrina and Daphne shared a knowing glance. They had made a pact with the former mayor to keep certain secrets—secrets they'd learned during a trip to the future. They were all determined to make sure that particular future never happened, but to do that they had to make sure history played out the way it was supposed to. Warning anyone about the dangers they were about to face might change their decisions, making it impossible to predict when tragedy would strike. But they wished they could at least tell the people they loved the truth.

"More secrets?" Ms. White guessed.

"We're trying to protect you, too," Daphne said.

"Everyone wants to protect Snow White. Well, I'm not a china doll, Daphne. I've been fighting my own battles for a long time."

There was a long silence before Snow finally spoke again. This time, her voice was as cool as the chilly air. "The three of you should get home. Relda is probably worried sick about you."

Then she turned, got into her car, and drove away.

Uncle Jake was thrilled with what the children had discovered at the library. Daphne wanted to write a letter to Goldilocks right away, but Uncle Jake said he had a better idea. He shared few details of his plan but told the girls he had made a call to some old friends who were sending something that would work a lot faster than a stamp and an envelope. In fact, he promised, it would change everything.

The girls watched Goldilocks through the mirror. She was riding in a long boat on a canal, gazing up at the moon.

Sabrina woke the next morning to shouting and pounding. She rubbed her eyes and looked around, not surprised to find that Daphne was sleeping soundly through the chaos. Sabrina slipped on her robe and stomped downstairs. At the front door, she found a creature that looked like it was part dwarf, part crocodile. It was poking its head out of the umbrella stand and gesturing to the door.

"There's a man at the north entrance," the creature hissed into a walkie-talkie. "Where's my backup? I need backup!"

Sabrina looked outside and found Robin Hood on the front porch. "That's just Robin Hood. He's a friend," Sabrina explained.

"Cancel that backup, people!" the creature shouted into his walkie-talkie. "We are back to code yellow. All clear. I repeat, we are at code yellow." Then, he vanished back into the stand.

Sabrina opened the door, and Robin barged in without as much as a hello.

"You're not dressed? Kid, you've got to get dressed!" the lawyer exclaimed. "Where is everyone?"

"In bed. It's not even eight in the morning," she said.

"Well, wake them! We have to get over to the courthouse now," Robin cried. "The trial is starting today!"

4

LITTLE JOHN AND I PETITIONED THE COURT TO hold a proper trial for Canis," Robin Hood explained as he hurried the family up the steps of the Ferryport Landing Municipal Courthouse. "To be honest, after our little run-in with Nottingham yesterday, I never guessed they would grant it. I assumed it was a lost cause until this morning, when one of the merry men was here filing a class-action suit and noticed the grand jury's schedule posted on the wall."

"Why wouldn't you have been informed of the trial ahead of time?" Granny Relda asked.

"Because Heart and Nottingham are trying to catch us off guard," Little John replied as they met him at the top of the stairs. "If they can present their case without anyone there to defend Canis, the trial could be over within minutes."

"So they're pulling a fast one," Uncle Jake said.

"Absolutely," Robin confirmed, "but they've forgotten how fast I can be. We'll put a stop to this."

"Do you have anything prepared?" Granny asked.

The lawyers shook their heads. "No, but there's nothing to worry about," Little John said. "We'll ask the judge for a postponement, and then we'll have plenty of time to prepare."

Sabrina saw Daphne take out her dictionary. "Daphne, *postponement* means that they want more time before the trial begins."

Daphne scowled. "I don't need your help."

Robin and Little John ushered the group into a courtroom. Sabrina was startled to find it packed with Everafters: goblins, witches, fairy godmothers, winkies, munchkins, and countless more. There were few empty seats left.

On the far side of the room was the jury box—two rows of seats set apart from the crowd. The jury was already present. It was made up of twelve Everafters, each more bizarre than the last: the Cheshire Cat, Glinda the (not-so) Good Witch, an enormous caterpillar smoking a hookah pipe, a talking sheep, a young man dressed entirely in blue, and, much to Sabrina's horror, an enormous egg with arms, legs, and a gnarly crack at the top of its shell. Sabrina recognized most of them from around town, but there was one juror whom she knew very well—Prince Charming.

"Granny, look!" Sabrina said, pointing.

The old woman had already seen him.

"Why is he on the jury?" Uncle Jake asked.

"I don't know," Granny said.

"Maybe he's trying to help Mr. Canis," Daphne said, but Sabrina wasn't so sure. Charming hated Canis with a passion. And he had very recently pledged his loyalty to the Scarlet Hand. It was unlikely he'd be on the Grimms' side.

Watching over the crowd were three guards with human limbs and heads but huge playing cards for bodies. Sabrina knew they acted as Mayor Heart's personal security, but now they seemed to be working for the courts, as well. The Five of Diamonds and the Seven of Spades watched the entryway, while the Nine of Diamonds guarded an oddly shaped man sitting on a raised platform at the front the room. He had a tremendous head and a mane of unruly gray hair. His nose was so obnoxiously large that Sabrina suspected Lilliputians could live in his nostrils. He wore a big black top hat and a long black robe, and he wielded a carpenter's hammer.

"Is that the judge?" Sabrina asked incredulously.

Granny's face paled. "Oh dear," she whispered. "This is not good news."

The cards guarding the entryway opened the doors, and several more soldiers entered. They filed in, dragging heavy chains shackled around Mr. Canis's wrists, ankles, and neck. He looked even more tired and filthy than the last time Sabrina had seen him, and there were several fresh wounds on his back and chest. The guards forced him into a seat, then ran the chains through an iron ring secured to the floor. Canis looked around at the crowd, growing angry when he spotted the Grimms.

"What are you doing here?" he growled.

"We came to help, of course," Granny Relda said.

"I don't want your help!"

"Order!" the judge demanded, pounding on his desk with the hammer. Sabrina thought judges used gavels, not real hammers— now she saw why. With each violent slam of the tool, splinters from the podium shot in all directions. "What is this commotion in my courtroom?"

Robin Hood and Little John rushed to the judge and bowed respectfully. "Your honor, we apologize to the court for our tardiness. We're counselors for Mr. Canis."

"Do you think you can show up for court whenever you want, counselors?" the judge roared. "I should have the two of you thrown out of here immediately."

The outburst caused the crowd to chatter excitedly, which enraged the judge even further. He slammed his hammer down again and again. "Order! I'll have order in this courtroom," he bellowed. "I want a toasted sesame bagel with low-fat scallion cream cheese. You folks can order whatever you want, but get separate checks."

Robin Hood and Little John exchanged a puzzled glance. "Your

Honor, we request a postponement," Robin Hood said. "We only just learned our client was being tried a half an hour ago."

"Your client wasn't tried a half an hour ago. He is being tried right now," the judge said matter-of-factly.

"Of course, Your Honor. What I mean is, my associate and I learned about the trial a half an hour ago."

"What trial a half an hour ago? I think the two of you should be concerned with the trial that is going on right now!"

Little John looked as if he might strangle the judge. "Your Honor. As I was saying, we wish to postpone this trial until we've had time to speak with our client about his defense, as well as to interview the prosecution's witnesses."

The judge turned beet red and slammed his hammer down violently. "Overruled!"

"But, Your Honor—" Robin begged.

"Why did you invite us down here if you weren't ready for the trial?" the judge moaned.

"Sir, we didn't invite you down here," Little John corrected.

"Well, that's terribly rude," the judge cried. "You put on a trial, and you don't have the common decency to invite me? Counselors, you are really not getting off to a good start."

"Has this guy lost his mind?" Sabrina asked.

"Yes," Uncle Jake whispered. "He's the Mad Hatter."

Sabrina's mouth fell open in disbelief. Even she knew the story of the Mad Hatter from *Alice's Adventures in Wonderland*. Alice met him at a tea party, and he nearly drove the poor girl insane. He was the very definition of crazy.

"How did a man like him get to be a judge?" Sabrina asked.

"I appointed him," a woman's voice said. Sabrina turned to find Mayor Heart sitting directly behind her. Her face was painted in bone white pancake makeup, dark ruby lipstick, and purple eyeshadow that reached the edge of her hairline. She looked like a deranged clown.

Sabrina wondered if she looked like that when she tried to put on her own makeup.

"This isn't fair," Sabrina seethed. "You can't have a madman running a courtroom."

"As a matter of fact, I can. You see, I'm the mayor," Heart replied with a wicked laugh. "Still, it doesn't matter who oversees the trial. I know how it's going to end. The Wolf will hang, and then there will be no one left to protect you, brat."

A commotion at the front of the room turned Sabrina's attention back to the trial itself.

"Where is the prosecuting attorney?" Judge Hatter demanded.

"I'm right here, Your Honor," a man shouted as he barreled into the courtroom.

"Bluebeard." Daphne gasped, along with most of the others in the courtroom. Sabrina cringed at the sight of him.

"I'm quite ready to get started if it pleases the court," Bluebeard said, opening his briefcase.

Robin Hood glared at Bluebeard. "I haven't had any time to discuss the case with my client. Nor have I interviewed any of your witnesses."

"That's unfortunate," Bluebeard said. "But I'm sure you'll catch up. As for right now, I'm ready to call my first witness. Rather, my first three witnesses. I'd like to call them all to the stand at the same time, if it pleases the court."

"Ooh, it might," Hatter said, grinning and clapping like a happy child. "Call your witnesses."

Robin and Little John tried to assure Mr. Canis that everything would be fine. The old man acted as if he couldn't hear them.

"The prosecution calls the Three Little Pigs to the stand," Bluebeard announced. The card guards opened the double doors, and in walked former police deputies Boarman and Swineheart. Both were portly but otherwise very distinct. Jed Boarman had curly brown hair and a moustache so thin, it appeared to have been drawn on with a pencil. He wore glasses and was prone to sweating profusely, especially when he was nervous. His friend and business partner Alvin Swineheart wore a pompadour haircut that reminded Sabrina of Elvis Presley. His long, bushy sideburns and reflective sunglasses added to the resemblance. Both men wore ill-fitting suits and ties. They scanned the courtroom as they entered and spotted

Sabrina and her family, flashing them apologetic smiles. *Were they going to say something that would hurt Mr. Canis's case?*

Their arrival sparked a lot of chatter in the courtroom. Hatter furiously banged his hammer, and when that didn't silence the crowd, he slammed his own forehead onto the podium. When the room was finally quiet, Bluebeard approached the witnesses.

"I was under the impression that there were three of you," he said.

Swineheart ran his hands through his slick hair. "Well, there are, but we're not attached at the hip, ya know."

"So, am I to understand that Ernest Hamstead won't be joining us? Where is your friend?"

Swineheart and Boarman suddenly changed into pigs, a transformation that indicated they were anxious or afraid. They squealed for a moment but quickly reverted to their human forms.

"We don't exactly know where he is," Boarman said sheepishly. "He's missing."

"Missing?" Bluebeard said. "How could someone go missing in a town this small?"

Boarman shrugged, not meeting Bluebeard's eyes.

"I suppose just the two of you will do," Bluebeard continued. "Gentlemen, will you tell us what you do for a living?"

"We're architects," Boarman said, "and retired deputies for the Ferryport Landing Police Department."

"Fascinating," Bluebeard said. "Now, I heard a story about the three of you, and I was wondering if you could tell me which parts are true and which parts are myth. I hope that'll be easy enough. Now, according to this story, the three of you had a run-in with the Big Bad Wolf. Is that correct?"

Boarman and Swineheart nodded.

"And if I've heard the story correctly, each of you built yourselves a home. One made a house out of straw, the other made a house of twigs, and the last—brick. Which one of you built which house?"

"I built the twig one," Swineheart said.

"And I built mine out of brick," Boarman replied.

Bluebeard smiled and turned to the jury. "I suppose it's safe to say that the missing Mr. Hamstead worked with straw. Now, I'm no architect, but I know a thing or two about houses. You have to build them out of strong materials. Straw and twigs are not going to pass building codes, but if you bribe the right officials, you might get away with it."

"I have never bribed anyone in my life!" Swineheart cried.

Bluebeard ignored him. "Bricks are a pretty sturdy material. However, very few people would choose to build a house out of straw, right?"

Boarman and Swineheart said nothing.

"Straw would fall down at the slightest wind. Straw would fall apart at the first rain. I could break into a straw house with a lawn mower!" Bluebeard shouted, causing even members of the jury to chuckle. "But, like I said, I'm no architect. Perhaps there's something to this straw house. Tell me what happened to your three houses."

Swineheart rolled his eyes impatiently. "The Wolf blew two of them down. The brick house survived his attack."

He bowed his head, seemingly regretting using the word *attack* when talking about Canis.

"How frightening! You must have thought you were dead for sure. Do you see the Wolf who did this in the courtroom today?" Bluebeard asked. He turned to face Mr. Canis with a wicked grin on his face.

"Nope," said the pigs.

Bluebeard's face fell, and he spun back around to the pigs. "I'm sorry, gentlemen," he said. "Perhaps you didn't hear me correctly. I asked if you see the Wolf in the courtroom."

"We heard you," Boarman said. "The answer is no."

"You don't see that wolf right over there?" Bluebeard asked as he pointed at Mr. Canis.

"That ain't the Wolf," Swineheart said matter-of-factly. "That's a fellow we know by the name of Mr. Canis."

"Don't play games with me!" Bluebeard bellowed, slamming his fist down on his table. "The Wolf and Mr. Canis are the same person."

"You're wrong, smart guy. They aren't the same person," Boarman corrected. "Mr. Canis is a kind, trustworthy man; the Wolf is a monster locked up inside him. If you put Mr. Canis on trial for crimes the Wolf committed, you're punishing the wrong person."

The audience erupted into chatter, but silence fell when Judge Hatter tossed his hammer through a window, shattering the glass.

"ORDER!"

"Fine, let me ask you this," Bluebeard pressed. "Would the two of you characterize yourselves as friends of the Wolf . . . I mean, Mr. Canis?"

"We're friendly," Boarman said.

"We're not hanging out at the ice-cream parlor together, but I'd say we have a lot of respect for him. We've helped one another out in the past," Swineheart explained.

"Would you say Ernest Hamstead is friends with Mr. Canis?"

"Ernest is very close with Canis's friend Relda Grimm," Boarman replied. "He spends a lot more time with the two of them than we do."

"So, Ernest is a good friend of Mr. Canis's?"

The pigs nodded.

"Your missing friend, Ernest Hamstead, is a good friend of Mr. Canis's?"

The courtroom was so quiet, you could hear people breathing.

It was obvious what Bluebeard was insinuating: Mr. Canis had killed Ernest Hamstead.

But Sabrina knew the truth. The third little pig was alive and well, living in New York City. Except no one in the town could know he had found a way past the magical barrier that trapped the rest of the Everafters in Ferryport Landing.

"This Mr. Hamstead is an interesting fellow. He built a house out of straw and was surprised at how easily it was demolished. Then, he befriended the monster who destroyed his property and tried to eat him. He sounds very trusting. Maybe a little too trusting," Bluebeard said as he turned to face Mr. Canis. "Tell me, monster, were you truly friends with him, or were you just biding your time, waiting for the day when you could finish him off?"

Mr. Canis snarled.

"Let's face it," Bluebeard continued, hovering over Mr. Canis. "Hamstead doesn't sound like the sharpest knife in the drawer. Did you make him trust you so you could finally kill and eat him like you did Little Red Riding Hood's defenseless old grandmother?"

"Objection!" Robin Hood shouted. "Mr. Canis is not on trial for killing Mr. Hamstead. There is no proof that Hamstead is even dead. Where is the body? Where is the murder weapon?"

"Murder weapon? Just look at the savage teeth on this brute!"

Bluebeard shouted. "And the body is probably still digesting in his belly!"

Mr. Canis roared with rage. He stood and swatted at his chair, knocking it against the wall. It exploded into splinters. A dozen card guards rushed at him, clubbing him with the hilts of their swords, but their blows didn't faze Canis. He threw them off, tossing them across the room. Reinforcements eventually arrived, and the guards managed to drag Canis from the courtroom.

Judge Hatter, who had pounded the podium with his fists, shoes, and head, slumped in his chair, wiping his sweaty face with his robes. "I think we've heard enough for today. We'll meet back here Tuesday."

"But, Your Honor," Bluebeard said. "Tuesday was yesterday."

"Hmmm . . . you may be right. We can't exactly meet in the past, can we?" he asked. "No, really, can we?"

He paused, waiting for an answer to his ridiculous question.

"When would you like to meet in the future?" he finally continued.

"Tomorrow?" Bluebeard offered.

"Very well, time marches on despite our best efforts. We shall meet tomorrow," Judge Hatter said.

"But your honor!" Little John cried. "We haven't had an opportunity to question the witnesses."

The judge ignored the protest and darted out of the room,

followed by several card guards. The Five of Diamonds dismissed the crowd, and everyone filed out through the double doors. As she left, Sabrina caught Mayor Heart talking to Prince Charming. The nasty woman was giggling like an idiot, flashing her crooked yellow teeth. "Better luck tomorrow," she cackled toward the Grimms.

Robin Hood looked bewildered. "What just happened?" he asked.

"We got steamrolled," Little John grumbled.

The family hadn't been home ten minutes before there was a knock at the door. Swineheart and Boarman stood on the porch looking sad and embarrassed.

"We know you didn't have a choice," Granny said after Sabrina invited them inside.

"We let him down," Swineheart said.

"I'm sure Mr. Canis knows you were trying to help. Please, boys, have a seat and I'll fetch some refreshments," Granny offered as she darted off into the kitchen.

"This trial is a travesty," Boarman complained. "We can't let Heart and Nottingham get away with this!"

"I don't know how we're going to stop them," Sabrina said. "Mayor Heart handpicked the judge, and there are several members of the Scarlet Hand on the jury."

"And Charming! What in the blazes is he doing in that crowd?" Swineheart asked.

"You know him as well as I do," Boarman said. "Charming is always an opportunist. He's on whichever side is winning."

"Perhaps the two of you could help us out," Granny said when she returned with a platter full of roast beef sandwiches, sauerkraut, pickles, baked beans, and egg salad. Sabrina couldn't believe how normal it all looked. Where was all the brightly colored bread and stinky, glowing gravy?

"Help?" Swineheart asked as he eyed the sandwiches hungrily.

"With our defense," Granny continued. "Today, they caught us off guard. We can't let that happen again. I believe the key to our success is preparation. We need to learn everything we can about Red Riding Hood, her grandmother, Mr. Canis, and anything else related to the crime. Unfortunately, there are hundreds of versions of the Red Riding Hood story. You two have known Canis a lot longer than we have, and I think you might be able to weed out the fiction from the facts."

"We'll do our best," Boarman said, "right after we have one of these delicious sandwiches."

Granny Relda let them eat as much as they wanted, refilling the platter more than a few times. Sabrina took a step back for her own safety. She had never seen anyone eat so much or with so much enthusiasm. Even Elvis winced at the tremendous amount of food Boarman and Swineheart consumed. The pigs ate and ate while sifting through the family's countless books. Sabrina, Daphne, Uncle Jake, and Granny helped with the search.

"What should we be looking for?" Boarman asked.

"Any kind of discrepancy," Granny replied.

Daphne whipped out her pocket dictionary. It would have been easy enough for Sabrina to tell the little girl that *discrepancy* was another word for *contradiction*, but Daphne didn't seem to want Sabrina's help anymore. It hurt that "grown-up" Daphne no longer needed her.

"It was six hundred years ago," Sabrina complained.

"Well, we should read them all, anyway," Granny said. "Maybe we'll find other eyewitnesses."

"I think all the eyewitnesses are in the Wolf's belly," Sabrina said.

Granny flashed her an angry look. The old woman was still giving Sabrina the cold shoulder after their spat the day before. The memory of Canis's outburst in the courtroom popped into Sabrina's head. His rage-filled eyes and horrible roar made her shudder. Was there anything human left in the old man, and if so, how long could it hold out against the monster? Even more unsettling was her family's lack of worry. What if the Wolf were to escape his chains in court or bust out of jail? Would he come back to Granny's house? What would the Grimms do if the Wolf showed up at their front door? What would they do if he lost his temper with them? It seemed as if she was the only one considering the dark possibilities.

While everyone else was searching through the books, Sabrina managed to corner Boarman and Swineheart in the kitchen, where they were rummaging in the refrigerator for more sandwiches. She made sure no one was listening and then carefully closed the kitchen door behind her.

"Mr. Hamstead is alive," she said.

"We know," Swineheart said. "He wrote us a letter. You know, the next time you folks leave town and want to bring along an Everafter, don't hesitate to call."

"Sorry, it was a last-minute thing," Sabrina said. "Did he also tell you he gave us the key?"

The men shared a nervous look.

"No, he didn't," Boarman replied.

"He said not to go get the weapon until we absolutely have to, but the way Mr. Canis is looking, I'd say it's high time. Mr. Hamstead said you two could teach us how to use it."

"What's there to teach?" Boarman asked. "It's pretty self-explanatory. Just don't point it at anything you don't want to destroy."

Swineheart chuckled. "You remember when Ernest accidentally aimed it at his Camaro? I heard they found it in the next county."

The pigs burst into laughter, both turning bright pink before they got themselves under control.

"You three were the only ones to beat the Wolf, right? Mr. Hamstead told us a little, and I've heard others mention it before, but I've never heard exactly what happened," Sabrina said.

Swineheart sighed. "Well, back before you were born, the Wolf marched through this town terrorizing people, and no one could stop him. Not even your Grandpa Basil could control him, and Basil was one of the smartest and toughest humans I've ever met. Now, a furry lunatic running around blowing people's houses down is the responsibility of the police department, but there wasn't much we could do. We organized a search party from time to time, got people together to try to find his den. I even had a witch fly me over the forest, in the hope that I would spot him from the air. We tried everything to trap him. We shot him with tranquilizer darts, even poisoned him, but he was always a step ahead of us. Everything we did was a major waste of time. He was too smart and too fast."

"The whole mess drove Charming crazy," Boarman added. "He said we looked foolish, and, worse, we were wasting taxpayer money. He thought he could solve every problem, so he went out looking himself. We found him a week later, hanging upside down from a tree. The Wolf had tied him up with his own rope. Charming was humiliated. But he was lucky to be alive, if you ask me."

"That explains why Charming and Canis don't like each other," Sabrina said.

Boarman nodded. "When we cut him down, Charming gave us a mandate: Stop the Wolf or stop coming to work. He was going to fire us if we didn't take the beast down. But we weren't a bunch of bumbling idiots. The Wolf was impossible to stop because he wasn't fighting fair. He was using a magic weapon, and the second you got close to him, he'd turn it on you, and *bam*! Game over! So, it was obvious to me that we had to get it away from him."

"Obvious to *you*, huh?" Swineheart said.

"Fine! We all came up with the idea," Boarman said, surrendering. "The point is, we were never going to have a chance to capture him until we could take his toy away. So we spread the word that Old MacDonald was concerned about how big his flock of sheep had grown. We knew the Wolf would come for the sheep, so we sat in MacDonald's barn and waited for him."

"Dressed as sheep," Swineheart said. "Definitely not my idea."

"I was going to leave out the embarrassing parts of the story," Boarman groaned.

"Don't sugarcoat it," Swineheart said.

"It all turned out OK. The Wolf never saw us coming. When he stormed into the barn, I hit him with a pickup truck," Boarman said.

"You ran him over?" Sabrina gasped.

"I had to! He's huge! If we'd had a tank, I would have used that. Luckily, the truck knocked the Wolf off his feet long enough for Hamstead to drop from the ceiling and snatch the weapon right out of his hand. You should have seen it, kid. We were like three fat little ninjas. Hamstead swung down on a rope. Swineheart smacked the Wolf with a shovel. I gunned the engine. It was a big day for pigs everywhere."

"And then you turned the weapon on him?"

"Heck no," Boarman said. "We ran."

"Wee-wee-wee, all the way home." Swineheart laughed. "We hopped into our squad cars and hightailed it out of there. I never saw the big guy so mad. He chased us all over Ferryport Landing before he finally gave up."

Boarman grinned from ear to ear. "Once we had the weapon, we practiced a few times, destroyed a few things accidentally, and prepared for the big showdown with the furball. The Wolf didn't disappoint. He charged into the police station with his teeth and claws, looking to turn us all into pork chops, but he got the beating of his life. I'm telling you, kid—the Three Little Pigs laid the smackdown on his furry behind."

"But when the smoke cleared, we found something none of us had expected," Swineheart added.

"What? Was it the weapon? Did it break or something?" Sabrina demanded, praying that the device, whatever it was, might still be in one piece.

"Oh, no, the weapon was just fine. It's just, well—we got a big surprise."

"What?"

"Mr. Canis," Boarman said.

"I'm confused," Sabrina said.

"So were we—still are, to a certain degree," Boarman explained. "Lying on the ground was a fully grown man who seemed to have appeared out of thin air. There was no such person as Mr. Canis before that fight. No one knew he existed. I assume Canis was the victim of some kind of curse or magic spell that turned him into the monster. Our town is filthy with people like that—Beast, the Frog Prince—you couldn't throw a rock without hitting someone who was turned into an animal at one point or another. Somehow, the weapon beat the Wolf so badly, it damaged the magic that gave the animal control over the body. Mr. Canis has been in charge ever since.

"Not that it has been easy. Poor old fellow didn't have any memories of who he was before that day. He didn't even know he'd been a monster. We could barely understand a word he said—rambling about witches and black winds invading his mind. We took him to your grandfather. Basil had a lot of experience with stuff like that, but it was Relda who decided to help him. She taught him all that yoga and meditation stuff, and soon he was able to tap into the Wolf's powers when he needed them without losing control over himself. Relda always believed Canis would be a great ally, and he's been living with your family ever since. It's only recently that he's been having trouble keeping the Wolf locked up inside of him."

Sabrina knew exactly what had happened to cause that trouble. Canis and Jack the Giant Killer had come to blows, and Canis had tasted Jack's blood. After that, the Wolf started taking over.

"So, this weapon you took from him will stop the Wolf. Could it—"

"Give Mr. Canis total control again?" Swineheart interrupted. "It might."

"And what is it? What is this weapon?"

Just then, Granny entered the kitchen with a tray of dirty dishes. "Oh dear. I had no idea there was anyone in here. I'm afraid we're dropping like flies. Jacob fell asleep an hour ago, and Daphne just dozed off herself. Gentlemen, why don't you two call it a night, as well? We appreciate everything you've done."

"Our pleasure," they assured her.

"Sabrina, could you help your sister into bed while I show our friends out?" Granny asked.

Sabrina was desperate to learn more about the weapon, but she knew she couldn't ask more questions in front of Granny. She said her good-byes and found Daphne asleep on the sofa. She helped her sister upstairs, out of her clothes and pearls, and into her pajamas.

Daphne mumbled something unintelligible when Sabrina crawled into bed beside her. A sliver of silver flashed in the dark, catching Sabrina's eye. The moonlight was reflecting off the key hanging around Daphne's neck.

For the second morning in a row, the Grimms woke to a loud banging on the front door. Sabrina hurried down the stairs, wishing Robin Hood wasn't such an early riser. But when she reached the bottom, her uncle rushed past her, crying, "It's here! It's here!" to the gathering family.

"What's here?" Daphne asked in between yawns.

Uncle Jake opened the door to a small spotted rabbit wearing a blue jacket and matching baseball cap. The uniform read TORTOISE AND HARE DELIVERIES WORLDWIDE . Accompanying him was a large green tortoise carrying an immense wooden chest on his shell.

When Daphne saw the animals, she squealed and bit the palm of her hand. "No way! You are so cute, I could eat you!" she cried, but when she saw Sabrina's amused smile, she hid her childish glee. "I mean . . . I'm pleased to meet you."

"You Jake Grimm?" the rabbit squeaked.

"Yes," Uncle Jake said.

"You gotta sign for this," the rabbit said, gesturing toward the box.

"You gotta take it off my back first," the tortoise groaned. "It weighs a ton!"

Uncle Jake took the box, placing it inside the door, and signed the rabbit's clipboard.

"What's in this thing, anyway?" the tortoise asked.

"Holiday gifts," Uncle Jake replied. "Thank you so much for bringing them by."

The animal duo didn't budge. The rabbit held out his paw and stared up at the family.

"I guess you probably have other deliveries to make," Uncle Jake continued, breaking the awkward silence.

"Yep," the tortoise said.

"Well, don't let us keep you," Jake said.

"Listen, pal. Let's not beat around the bush," the hare said. "It's customary to tip for a delivery, especially a backbreaking shipment like this one. We brought this thing all the way from the truck, and we got it here fast. I could have had my partner deliver it, but you wouldn't have gotten it until next year. You know how long a tortoise takes to deliver a package?"

"Long time, pal," the tortoise said.

"A real long time. Express service deserves a little thank-you, don't you think? I mean, I got a big family. I'm talking really big."

"He's a rabbit," the tortoise said by way of an explanation.

"Of course," Uncle Jake said, digging in his pockets. He pulled out a wadded-up five-dollar bill and stuffed it into the rabbit's shirt pocket.

"Thanks, pal. Oh, there's one more thing. You're gonna need this," the rabbit said as he took off his cap. Underneath was a long brass key, which he handed to Uncle Jake. "Have a nice day, and remember to use THDW."

"We get it there at any speed you need," the tortoise said.

The rabbit turned and snatched up the tortoise's back legs like he was a wheelbarrow, and together they waddled back to their truck.

"What's this?" Sabrina asked.

"You'll see," Uncle Jake said. "Get dressed, get your grandmother, and meet me in Mirror's room."

Ten minutes later, they found him kneeling over the chest in front of Mirror. "So, girls, remember when I said I'd found a better way to communicate with Goldilocks than just a letter?"

The girls nodded.

"Well, this is it!" Uncle Jake announced. "Goldilocks keeps moving from one place to the next, faster than we could ever get a letter into her hands. So I called some old friends for help, and they sent us this."

"What is it?" Sabrina asked.

"It's called the traveler's chest," Uncle Jake said.

"The traveler's what?" Sabrina asked.

Granny marveled at the chest. "Oh my. Your father used to talk about this, but I always thought he was pulling my leg."

"Nope, it's real. The Andersen triplets tracked it down a few years back and agreed to lend it to us. It's going to help us get to Goldilocks," Uncle Jake said.

"The Andersen triplets?" Daphne asked.

"The last living descendants of Hans Christian Andersen. They're magic hunters. They've got all kinds of stuff like this. I worked with them for a few years while I was away. We got into a lot of scrapes together, but it was fun."

Sabrina examined the chest. "How does it work?"

Uncle Jake used the brass key to open the lock on the front and then lifted the lid. The box was completely empty—not even a speck of dust.

"An old empty chest is going to help us find Goldilocks?" Daphne asked.

"Oops," Uncle Jake said as he closed the lid. "I forgot to tell it where I want to go."

"I'm confused," Daphne said.

"You tell the chest where you want to travel, and it will take you there. Anywhere! Watch!" Uncle Jake said. "Chest, I want to go to the Hotel Cipriani at Giudecca 10 in Venice, Italy."

Sabrina and Daphne shared a worried glance.

"I think he's finally lost it," Daphne said.

"It was bound to happen sooner or later," Sabrina added.

He turned the key in the lock and lifted the lid again. This time there was a spiral staircase inside, leading down, down, down. Sabrina felt the familiar tingle of magic under her skin.

"We're going to find Goldilocks!" Daphne cried, climbing in and pulling her sister behind her.

Uncle Jake nodded. "Mom, do you want to come along?"

Sabrina could see her grandmother's nervous face over the edge of the chest. "You know one of us has to stay in town."

"Technically, Henry and Veronica are fulfilling that obligation," their uncle said, tilting his head toward the girls' sleeping parents.

"Thanks, but no. I'm going to bake some muffins for Robin and Little John. I want to do something nice to say thank you for all their help." Granny said. "Be careful—girls, do what your uncle tells you to do, and stick together."

The house vanished as Sabrina descended the stairs, as did the light. Soon, she found herself in pitch-black darkness. Uncle Jake took a small red amulet from one of his coat pockets. He whispered something into it, and it illuminated their path.

"The amulet of the sun is one of the few magical items I have left after Baba Yaga stole my old coat," he complained. "There's a lot of empty pockets in the new one. I wonder if the Andersens might lend me a few more things to fill them up."

The family continued downward, step after step, until Sabrina began to fear there was no bottom to the stairs. She was about to suggest they turn back when she slammed into something hard.

"Could someone have warned me there's a door down here?" she complained.

"Sorry," Uncle Jake said. "Open it, but don't step through until you've looked both ways. The traveler's chest can be a little imprecise about where it lets you out, and that door leads into the real world. Anything could be on the other side."

Sabrina opened the door and found a sidewalk bustling with pedestrians. A canal was to her left, filled with gondolas. Tourists were snapping pictures of everything, but no one seemed to notice her or the portal.

"Looks all clear!" she said as she stared ahead. There, towering high, was the Hotel Cipriani.

"Let me see," Daphne said, pushing past Sabrina and out through the door. A moment later, Sabrina heard a huge splash and Daphne's voice.

"Help!"

5

SABRINA RUSHED THROUGH THE PORTAL AND found her sister bobbing up and down in a canal. She nearly fell in herself, but Uncle Jake pulled her back just in time.

The canal was filled with gondolas; men dressed all in white steered them with tall poles. One used his pole to nudge Daphne to the bank of the canal, where Uncle Jake fished her out.

When she was safely on land, Daphne reached into her pocket for her dictionary, but the book was waterlogged and ruined. Her face crinkled up in frustration, and she tossed the dictionary into a nearby trash can. "What does *imprecise* mean?" she huffed.

"It means not exact," Sabrina said.

Daphne scowled.

"You should have let me go first," Sabrina said.

Daphne scowled harder, wringing out her hair.

"Welcome to Venice, girls," Uncle Jake said.

Sabrina looked around and realized Scarecrow had been right about everything. There weren't any streets in Venice, at least not in this part of the city. Instead, there were canals lined by narrow sidewalks. The entrances to elegant hotels, apartments, and shops on either side of the canals were built high so that the water never touched the doorways. Boats of various shapes and sizes sailed by: Some were taxis, and others were for tourists to take on romantic rides beneath the majestic arches and bridges of the city. As a native New Yorker, Sabrina was rarely impressed with anyplace outside of the Big Apple. After all, once a person had seen the Statue of Liberty or had one of Nathan's hot dogs at Coney Island, there was little reason to see the rest of the world. But even she had to admit that Venice was awe inspiring.

"So, where's Goldilocks?" Daphne asked.

"There," Uncle Jake said, pointing at a beautiful woman standing on a balcony of the hotel. She wore tight blond curls, a sun-kissed tan, and a warm smile. She, too, was gazing out at the amazing city.

Sabrina was overwhelmed with emotion. For months, the girls had believed their parents abandoned them, only to discover they had been kidnapped. Rescuing them had provided little comfort, since they were both asleep under a powerful spell. The only way to break the spell was a romantic kiss, but since they were both unconscious, there didn't seem to be a way to make it happen. The only hope was Henry's first love, Goldilocks, and now that obstacle was almost hurdled, too. Hope, wonder, and joy were building in Sabrina's heart, threatening to explode like a shaken bottle of soda pop. Sabrina's feelings were mirrored in her sister's face. Daphne was grinning from ear to ear.

"Congratulations, girls," Uncle Jake said. "I think we're about to put the long family tragedy behind us. Let's go get our Goldie."

The trio raced into the hotel's busy lobby, which was even more beautiful than its exterior. The floors were made from sparkling marble. Opulent arches framed the doors, and stunning sculptures decorated the room. Dozens of bellhops rushed to and fro, carrying expensive luggage and helping guests to their rooms.

Unfortunately, the group's arrival did not go unnoticed. A chubby, gray-haired man in a black suit approached them with a disapproving frown. Sabrina realized how odd they must have looked in such an elegant place, her sister dripping wet and her uncle in his wrinkled blue jeans and bizarre overcoat.

"*Posso aiutarvi?*" he said.

"I'm sorry, we don't speak Italian," Uncle Jake said.

The man's frown deepened. "Americans," he huffed. "Are you lost?"

"No, we're looking for a guest of the hotel," Uncle Jake said.

"What is this guest's name?"

"Goldilocks," Sabrina said, expecting him to laugh in her face.

"Goldilocks," he said impatiently. "You are friends with Ms. Locks?"

Uncle Jake nodded. "Yes, we're very close."

The hotel manager shook his head in disbelief. "I'm afraid I can't help you. Please leave the—"

"No problem, pal," Uncle Jake said, "we'll just start knocking on doors until we find her. C'mon, girls."

The man's eyes widened in horror. "Absolutely not! Take those elevators along the east wall. She's on the third floor—suite three-eleven."

The group took the elevator up, then hurried down the elegant hallway until they found Goldilocks's room. There, they paused.

"This is it," Daphne said, taking Sabrina's hand. "I've been practicing what I'm going to say to Mom and Dad when they wake up."

"Sabrina, why don't you do the honors?" Uncle Jake gestured to the door with a smile.

Sabrina took a deep breath and knocked on the door. It drifted open at her touch. The lock and doorjamb were broken and splintered.

The Grimms looked at one another, suspicious.

Uncle Jake's face fell. "Stay here," he whispered, then stepped into the room. "Hello?"

There was no answer, but Sabrina heard the sound of breaking glass. Uncle Jake held up his hand to motion for everyone to be quiet. A door slammed, and he darted toward the sound. The girls exchanged a silent glance, then chased after him. He wasn't going to leave them in the hall if there was trouble.

Inside the beautiful suite, they found Uncle Jake holding his ear to a closed door.

"I told you to stay put," he said when they appeared.

"We heard you," Daphne said.

"We just didn't listen," Sabrina added.

Uncle Jake swung open the door to find a tall man in a black jacket and pants. He was wearing a black motorcycle helmet that hid his face, but on his chest was a horrible mark: a handprint in red paint. It was the mark of the Scarlet Hand.

The man punched Uncle Jake hard in the face and rushed past the girls, out of the room, and into the hallway. Sabrina and Daphne helped their uncle to his feet.

"That wasn't very cool," Jake complained as he rubbed his jaw.

"Who was that?" Sabrina asked.

"I have no idea," Uncle Jake said.

"Where's Goldilocks?"

They raced around the suite, but there was no sign of the blond beauty.

"She must have left before that guy showed up," Uncle Jake said. "But her clothes and suitcase are still in the closet."

Sabrina heard a loud engine rev outside. Everyone rushed to the balcony. The masked villain was sitting astride a black motorcycle. He revved his engine once more, then tore off with screeching tires along the narrow sidewalks running beside the canal. Goldilocks was drifting away in a gondola.

"There she is, and he's chasing her!" Daphne exclaimed.

"C'mon!" Uncle Jake cried. They flew down the stairs, across the lobby, and out the hotel's front doors. Once outside, Sabrina scanned the canal for Goldilocks. She was surprised how far the boat had traveled in such a short time.

"What now?" she asked, but Daphne was already jumping into an empty gondola. The others joined her, and after a few awkward attempts, Uncle Jake had the boat floating down the canal in pursuit of the mysterious Goldilocks. A few moments after pushing off, Sabrina heard angry shouts from the bank and turned to see a red-faced gondolier shaking his fist.

"I guess this is his boat," Sabrina said.

Daphne waved at the man apologetically. "Sorry! It's an emergency."

All the while, the man on the motorcycle crept along the sidewalks and bridges, like a tiger stalking its prey. His disruptive presence turned the heads of tourists and locals alike, as the sidewalks were meant for pedestrians only. On more than one occasion he forced an unlucky person to leap into the water to avoid being run over. In the canals, boats steered out of the way to avoid colliding with the unexpected swimmers. Other boats stopped abruptly, causing a traffic jam. In a matter of seconds, the family's chase came to a complete halt.

"What now?" Sabrina asked, watching Goldie's boat sailing farther and farther away.

"We improvise," Uncle Jake said, dropping the pole into the boat. He stood, nearly capsizing everyone, then stepped onto the boat next to them. Daphne and Sabrina were right behind him. They leaped from one boat to the next, each step causing them to bob up and down like they were walking on the moon. Soon they closed the gap between themselves and Goldilocks.

Daphne called out to Goldilocks when they were just three boats away. Goldilocks turned to them, but she was quickly distracted. The motorcyclist had parked his bike on a bridge directly over the canal. It was under construction, and several large stones intended for the repairs were stacked nearby. The man heaved one off the bridge, into Goldilocks's boat. It blasted through the boat's bottom, and water rocketed upward through the hole like a geyser. Startled, the gondolier leaped into the canal, leaving Goldilocks to fend for herself.

Goldilocks, however, stood up calmly and did something so strange, Sabrina began to question her sanity. Goldie chirped and squawked at a pigeon resting on the bridge. The bird seemed just as surprised by the woman's odd noises as Sabrina, and it flew away.

"What was that all about?" Sabrina asked, but before anyone could explain, the pigeon returned with a flock of others, casting an enormous shadow over the canal. They swooped down to Goldie's boat and hooked their tiny talons into her clothes. Then, together, they lifted her out of the sinking gondola and flew her high above the canals, over the hotels, and out of sight.

"That did not just happen!" Sabrina cried.

"She must have been talking to those birds. They seemed to understand her!" Daphne said.

"Yeah, I forgot she could do that," Uncle Jake said. "It's a handy skill when you're about to be dinner for three bears."

Sabrina looked around for the motorcyclist, but he was gone, too. The sound of his engine faded in the distance.

"Who was that guy, anyway?" Daphne asked as their gondola bumped into another, startling a pair of honeymooners.

"I don't know," Uncle Jake said. "But now we know why Goldie keeps moving around so much. The Scarlet Hand is chasing her."

When the family returned home, there was no time to discuss what had just happened. Granny Relda and Barto the miniature orc were waiting anxiously.

"Judge Hatter moved the trial up by three hours," Granny explained. "If we don't leave for the courthouse right now, we'll miss the day's proceedings."

The courtroom was even more crowded than it had been the day before. Word of the trial was spreading, and curious Everafters were clamoring for front-row seats. A hundred mice were scattered around the floor sitting in tiny folding chairs. A crowd of witches brought their own popcorn.

"They're treating this like it's some kind of show," Granny hissed.

"Stay close, people," Barto insisted as he pushed the crowds aside.

They passed Snow White on their way in. She smiled politely, and Sabrina waved. Granny thanked her for coming, though their conversation was stiff and awkward.

"Mr. Canis is in my prayers," she told the family, then drifted away to find a seat.

Briar Rose waved the Grimms over to a row near the front, where she had saved seats. When Uncle Jake sat next to her, she kissed him on the cheek. He returned the gesture by kissing her hand. Briar's fairy godmothers shot him angry looks, but he just laughed and offered them kisses, as well.

"Don't worry," he whispered to the princess. "I'll win them over."

"I know. Just like you did with me," she said, taking his hand.

Robin and Little John came over to say hello. They warned the family that the trial would be even more difficult than it had been the day before, and they were, unfortunately, proven right.

Bluebeard called witness after witness, seemingly finding everyone the Wolf had victimized over the course of hundreds of years. There was a steady stream of talking lambs, pigs, and assorted forest creatures. Little Bo Peep, complete with her flock, explained her heartbreak when she discovered her "lost" sheep had actually been eaten by the Wolf. As the day dragged on, Sabrina wondered if there was a single Everafter in Ferryport Landing that the Wolf had not tried to devour. She watched Canis closely, waiting for another outburst, but he sat quietly without incident.

The only outbursts came from his lawyers. Like the day before, Judge Hatter refused Robin and Little John the chance to ask their own questions. Nottingham and Mayor Heart watched everything with amusement, openly cackling whenever the judge denied Robin's requests or ignored his objections.

"Does the prosecution have any more witnesses today?" Judge Hatter asked.

"We are finished for today, Your Honor," Bluebeard replied.

Robin leaped up. "Are we going to get a chance to cross-examine the witnesses?"

Judge Hatter rose to his feet. "Let's meet in the morning."

He strolled out of the courtroom, ignoring Robin and Little John's protests.

"This is outrageous!" Little John bellowed, knocking over his chair.

"Yes, it is, isn't it?" the sheriff said cheerfully.

Little John looked like he might lunge at Nottingham, but Robin Hood held him back. "He's not worth the headache, my friend."

Nottingham laughed darkly, then left the courtroom with Mayor Heart. The crowd of onlookers followed.

"How can you do this?" Snow's voice rang out across the crowd. When Sabrina finally spotted her, she was standing in front of Charming, jabbing her finger into his chest.

"Snow, this is none of your business," he said quietly.

"None of my business?" she snapped. "This is everyone's business. How can you turn your back on this town and throw yourself in with the Scarlet Hand? And how can you sit on this jury that's trying to put Canis to death? What is going on in your head? I can't believe I wanted to marry you. I don't even know you!"

Without a word, Charming turned his back on her and left the room.

Bluebeard rushed to Snow's side, shoving people out of his way to get to her. He grabbed her by the wrist and whispered something in her ear. Sabrina couldn't hear what he was saying, but Ms. White paled, her expression shifting from furious to anxious.

"What should we do?" Daphne asked.

"Don't worry," Barto said. He barked a couple of orders into his walkie-talkie. Suddenly, a battalion of little green trolls raced into the room and tackled Bluebeard. He swatted at them viciously, but there were too many. Taking advantage of the distraction, Snow rushed out of the courtroom, thanking Barto for his help.

"Just doing my job," Barto said. "The boss said security extends to friends of the Grimms. If you felt it appropriate to mention this to Puck, I'd be most grateful, I would."

When Snow was gone, Sabrina turned her attention back to Granny Relda. The old woman was busy trying to rebuild Robin's and Little John's confidence.

"You're doing your best."

"Our best is not going to keep your friend alive," Little John grunted.

"I agree," Robin said. "We need our own witness, someone who was there when Red walked in on the Wolf."

"It was six hundred years ago," Sabrina reminded them.

"There is one eyewitness still around," Granny said.

"Mom," Uncle Jake said, "you don't mean—"

"Aww, no!" Daphne cried. "Not her!"

Granny nodded. "We need to go talk to Red Riding Hood."

After she and her "pet" Jabberwocky had wreaked havoc on the town, Red Riding Hood was admitted to the mental-health wing of Ferryport Landing Memorial Hospital. Since Red had proven to be a volatile patient, witches cast a magical barrier around her room. It allowed doctors and nurses to visit, but it prevented Red from wandering the halls or, worse, escaping the hospital altogether. Sabrina didn't have a lot of faith in the spell. Red had managed to escape a similar one in the past, with disastrous results, but so far, the little girl had stayed put.

When the group arrived, Sabrina could sense that much of the hospital staff shared her jitters. There were only a few people working in the mental-health wing, but they looked tired, with dark circles under their eyes and unkempt hair. The slightest noise caused them to jump and sent a few into hysterics. Perhaps it was their terrifying Everafter patient that had them so run-down, but Sabrina suspected the abandoned halls weren't helping. With so many humans gone from the town, Ferryport Landing Memorial felt deserted.

A nurse named Sprat met them at the door. "The child is quite popular this week," she said. "You're her second group of visitors in the same number of days."

"Bluebeard?" Robin Hood asked.

"How did you know?" Nurse Sprat replied. "Creepy guy, that one. I can't stand to be alone with him for longer than a minute. He and Red are like two peas in a pod, if you ask me."

"Did you hear what they talked about, Nurse Sprat?" Little John asked.

"Nope. Truth is, I try to stay as far away from her as I can."

"We're aware of her troubles. What kind of treatment is she receiving here? Drugs? Counseling? Group therapy?" Robin asked.

"Treatment?" Nurse Sprat asked. "There's no treatment for a brain like hers. Not that I blame her for the way she acts. Poor thing. I'd probably have a couple screws loose, too, if my grandmother had been eaten by a wild animal."

The nurse led them down a long, bright hallway and stopped outside of a door with the words MEDICAL PERSONNEL ONLY painted in bright red lettering. At least a dozen heavy-duty locks secured it. Obviously, the staff held as little faith in the barrier spell as Sabrina. When Nurse Sprat was finished unlocking the door, she opened it and stepped aside.

"If I hear you screaming, I promise I'll come running."

"Thanks," Sabrina said, unconvinced.

"Oh, and keep your fingers in your pockets. She's a biter," Nurse Sprat said, closing the door behind them.

"Perhaps I should guard the door," Barto said, peering nervously into Red's room.

"Some security," Sabrina grumbled.

Robin Hood led the group into a bright white room with prison bars on the windows and walls lined with thick, rubber padding. Crayons and colored pencils were scattered about, many smashed underfoot and smeared on the floor. Dozens of drawings were taped to the walls, all depicting the same scene: a small house in the woods before which stood a mother, a father, a grandmother, a Jabberwocky, and a small girl in a red cloak. The mother was carrying a baby in her arms.

Red Riding Hood sat at a tiny pink table bolted to the floor. She was having a tea party with several dolls, all of which were mangled and beaten. Most were missing their eyes, others legs and arms.

"Relda, if you'd like to ask the questions, feel free," Little John said, eyeing the girl nervously.

"Of course," Granny said. "I've had some experience with Red."

"Yeah, like that time she tried to kidnap you and kill us," Sabrina said.

"*Lieblings*, stay close," Granny said to the children.

The group approached the table tentatively, like they were sneaking up on a gorilla.

"Party guests!" Red Riding Hood cried when she noticed them. She clapped her hands and laughed. "Please, have a seat. There's plenty of tea and cake."

"It's a lovely party," Granny Relda said, sitting. She was followed by Daphne, Robin Hood, and then Little John. Sabrina was happy to stand. She didn't want to get too close to the little girl.

"Thank you. Would you care for a cookie?" Red Riding Hood asked as she gestured to an empty plate at the center of the table. "My grandmother made them."

"Thank you," the old woman replied. She reached over and pretended to take one of the cookies. Robin and Little John did the same, while Red Riding Hood poured imaginary tea into everyone's cups.

"Red, how are you enjoying your stay at the hospital?" Granny asked.

"They took my basket," the little girl said. "I need my basket. I have to take it to my grandmother's house. She's very ill."

"I'm sure they will give it back to you," Granny assured her.

"Right now, you need to focus on getting some rest. I hope you don't mind, but I'd like to ask you some questions," Robin said as he pretended to sip his tea.

"Everyone has questions," Red said. "So many questions. The people in the white coats ask them all day, but when I answer, they tell me it's my imagination. And they won't answer any of mine. They're very rude."

"Well, how about if we play a little game? You can ask me a question, and I will try to answer it, and then I'll ask you a question, and you can do the same," Granny Relda said.

"Games! I love games!" Red said as she clapped her hands. "Me first!"

"Very well, what is your question?" Granny replied, as Robin Hood turned on his tape recorder.

"Where is my kitty?" Red asked.

Granny looked to the girls for help. She didn't understand Red's question, but Sabrina knew all too well what Red wanted to know. "Kitty" was what Red called the Jabberwocky, a fearsome, deadly creature with a thousand teeth. The family had used an enchanted sword known as the Vorpal blade to kill it.

"Your kitty is sleeping," Sabrina said.

"Sleeping?"

"Yes, he went to sleep and he didn't wake up," Granny said, suddenly understanding.

"Oh," Red said, falling quiet for a moment. "I love my kitty."

"Perhaps you could get a new one," Robin Hood said.

"A smaller one with less teeth," Sabrina replied.

"One that doesn't breathe fire," Daphne added.

"Your turn!" Red announced, suddenly rebounding from her melancholy.

"What can you tell us about the Big Bad Wolf?" Robin asked.

Red Riding Hood stared at him for a long moment. She was obviously confused.

"He means the doggy," Sabrina added, recalling the word Red had used to describe Mr. Canis. "You remember the doggy, right?"

"Oh, yes! The doggy," Red said. "I loved the doggy, but he was bad."

"Bad?"

"Very bad. He bit Grandma," Red said.

"That's not very nice," Granny Relda said. "We were wondering what you remember about the night the doggy bit your grandma."

The little girl sat quietly for a moment. She stared into the distance as if she were struggling to remember something. "Cages," she said softly, then looked around the room. "So many cages. My turn!"

Uncle Jake turned to Granny Relda. "What cages?"

Granny shook her head. "I've read nearly every version of the story, and I've never seen any mention of cages."

"Red, can you tell us more about these cages?" Robin Hood asked.

"NO!" the child shrieked. There was so much rage in her voice, it startled even Little John. He nearly fell off his chair. "It was my turn to ask a question. You have to play the game right."

"Of course, you're right," Granny said as calmly as possible. "We didn't mean to skip your turn."

The rage melted off Red's face; it was as if it had never been there at all. "Can I go home?"

Sabrina shuddered. The last thing Ferryport Landing needed was Red Riding Hood walking free.

"Red, you're very sick, and you need to get better," Granny Relda said kindly. "Once that happens, you can leave the hospital."

"I don't feel sick. I don't have a runny nose."

"That's because it's your mind that has the runny nose. It's a different kind of illness. You can't feel it at all."

Red frowned.

"Now it's my turn," Granny said. "Can you tell us about the cages?"

"The doggy was in one because he was very bad, and Granny did a dance all around them, and then there was wind, and then the doggy went into the man with the ax and he was angrier than the doggy ever was. He made the other man scared and he cried," Red said in one breath. "My turn! Have you seen my baby brother?"

Sabrina was exhausted listening to the child's rambling stories. Talking to her seemed like a tremendous waste of time. Nothing she said made any sense.

Even Granny was confused. "I didn't know you had a baby brother, Red."

"Oh, yes," the girl cooed. "He's got bright red hair, pink skin, and big green eyes. I just love him so much. I left him in his crib. I'm sure he needs his bottle."

Sabrina and Daphne shared a knowing look. They had suspected that this baby brother of Red's wasn't really a relative, but a child she and the Jabberwocky had kidnapped. But, having seen her tea party, Sabrina wondered if Red was talking about another toy doll. They'd found a crib and baby toys in the abandoned asylum where Red had once lived, but no sign of an actual baby.

"Oh, yes," Granny lied. "He's perfectly safe."

"Good. He's a very sweet baby." Red sighed. "Your turn."

"I'd like to talk more about the night the doggy bit your grandmother, Red," Robin said. "You said there were two men in your grandma's house, right?"

Red nodded. "One was the doggy. One was the man."

"This is pointless," Sabrina whispered to her grandmother. "She is so confused—how can we trust anything she says?"

Granny nodded reluctantly. "I'm afraid I agree. Perhaps we should go."

"Will you come and visit me again?" the little girl asked.

Sabrina cringed, as did Daphne. Red unnerved the both of them.

"We'll try," Granny said. "In the meantime, you work on getting better."

"Tell the doggy to be good," Red said. "Good doggies get treats."

Nurse Sprat let them out, then went to work refastening the various locks and bolts that kept Red safely away from others.

"What's wrong?" the nurse asked the lawyers when she noticed their puzzled faces.

"Something isn't adding up here," Robin said.

"I agree. I know that story inside and out, and it isn't anything like the one she just told us," Uncle Jake said.

"I don't recall anything about cages or the presence of two men," Granny said. "Do you suppose the story is not as close to the actual event as everyone believes?"

"I wouldn't be doing my job if I didn't try to find out," Robin said. "I think we need to visit your furry friend again, Relda. I'm betting there's something about that day he's not telling us."

"Agreed," Little John said. "But I think we'll need a little help from the princess this time."

Uncle Jake dropped his mother, the girls, Robin Hood, and Little John off at the jailhouse. He needed to get back to Mirror to track down Goldilocks.

"Nottingham is never going to let us see Mr. Canis again," Daphne said as they approached the jailhouse.

Robin Hood smiled. "I agree, but I have an idea."

He heaved a trash can off the ground and sent it sailing through the front window of a jewelry store. An alarm bell wailed.

"What are you trying to do?" Sabrina cried. "Get us arrested?"

"Hide!" Robin shouted, and the group hurried around the corner of the jailhouse and ducked behind some bushes. Seconds later, they watched Sheriff Nottingham rush into the street. He spotted the broken window and let loose a series of curse words that caused Granny to cover Daphne's ears. Then, Nottingham dashed into the store.

"Let's go," Robin said, and together everyone raced into the jailhouse.

They stormed into the room with the cells. There, they found Mr. Canis slumped in the corner, breathing hard and tending to fresh wounds. He looked tired and even more wolflike than he had at the courthouse.

"Why have you come?"

"We spoke to Red," Granny Relda explained.

Canis growled. "You're wasting your time, Relda. Can't you see your efforts are all for nothing? I do not want to be set free. I am a danger to everyone."

"If we don't prove your innocence, they are going to put you to death," Robin said.

"As they should, outlaw. I am guilty."

"Are you certain?"

Canis studied Robin curiously.

"Red told us some things about that day in her grandmother's home that don't add up. Plus, you yourself claim to have little memory of the event. Who really knows what happened?"

"I KNOW!" Canis roared. "I have spent my life making amends for my crimes. I will not pretend I did not commit them. I would rather die."

Granny Relda's face turned red, and she angrily waved her finger at the old man. "Mr. Canis, you better start talking right now, or I swear I'll . . . I'll . . . well, I don't know, but you won't like it!"

"C'mon, Canis," Robin said. "You can at least answer some questions."

"Fine," Canis said. "What do you want to know?"

"Let's start with what you remember," Robin said.

Canis sat quietly for a long time, then sighed. "Nothing. The day is a blur to me."

"Old friend!" Granny snapped.

"Relda, I swear I have no recollection of that day or many days after. I can see only tiny moments of my time as the Wolf, snapshots of grisly events. I remember the blood. I remember screams. But nothing is clear."

"Do you remember the house?" Robin asked.

"Vaguely," he admitted. "I remember running toward it."

"Red Riding Hood mentioned that it was full of cages when she arrived that day. She says you were in one of them. Do you remember that?" Robin said.

Canis shook his head. "The child is ill. I wouldn't take what she says too seriously. The damage I've done to that poor girl's mind is inexcusable."

Sabrina heard a terrific racket in the hallway and gasped, sure that Nottingham had returned. The door flew open to reveal Little John, carrying a woman in a blue gown over his shoulder. She held a miniature pug in her arms, and the little dog barked and snarled at the enormous lawyer.

"John, you put me down this minute!" she cried. "I am royalty, you know. I have never been so offended in my life."

Robin looked up into the woman's face. "Hello, Princess."

"Robin, so help me, if your lummox doesn't let me go—"

"Of course." Robin chuckled. "Set her down, friend."

Little John placed the princess on her feet. She straightened her pearls and complained bitterly about her wrinkled dress. Sabrina recognized her immediately. It was Beauty, wife to the infamous Beast. Though the couple were night and day in appearance, they shared a selfish entitlement and weren't above lying and cheating to get what they wanted. Beast was a member of the Scarlet Hand now, but Sabrina couldn't recall if Beauty was among their ranks, as well.

The little pug sniffed the air and yipped. The creature was wearing a little black doggy tuxedo, with a pocket square that matched Beauty's dress, as well as a tiny top hat. "Hush, Mr. Wuggles!" Beauty said, speaking to the dog in baby talk in an effort to calm him down. Soon, she spotted the family. "What are the Grimms doing here?"

"They're my clients," Robin said. "And they are in need of your special skills. I'm told you have a talent for soothing savage beasts."

Beauty peered into the cell. Her eyes grew wide, and she shook her head. "Robin Hood, you've lost your mind if you think—"

"You're the only hope we have," Robin said.

"But that's the—he's dangerous!"

"We know, but your husband was just as wild as the Wolf when you met him."

"My husband was never this wild," the princess protested. "I don't even know if it will work."

"If I thought we could get the information any other way, I wouldn't have asked you. C'mon, you owe me one."

"Fine! But this is it, Robin. No more favors."

"You're a peach, Beauty."

"What's she going to do?" Sabrina asked.

"I can tame wild animals, even put them into hypnotic states," Beauty replied, shoving her dog into Sabrina's hands. "OK, pal," she said to Canis. "I'm going to come in there, but you have to promise not to eat me."

Canis nodded.

Little John jingled a set of keys. "Easy enough. Nottingham left them behind when he ran out of here."

The cell door swung open, and Beauty stepped inside. "Close the door," she said.

Canis looked to Granny Relda with a doubtful expression.

"For me, old friend," Granny begged.

He threw up his hands in surrender. "Lock it, too."

Little John did as he was told. Beauty sat down on Canis's filthy cot and rested her hand on his muscular arm. All at once, the tension in his body seemed to melt away. He relaxed, and the strange, feral scent disappeared from the room. His eyes clouded with a calm, almost sleepy expression.

"Feel better?" the princess asked.

Canis nodded.

"Good. I want you to focus on my voice. It's the only thing you can hear. You will see only what I ask you to see, and it will appear before your eyes, like you are watching a movie," she said, then turned to the lawyers. "All right, he's ready."

"Ask him to describe what happened the night Red Riding Hood's grandmother died," Robin replied.

"Eww, that's going to be so gross," Beauty complained. She pointed at Sabrina. "You, cover Mr. Wuggles's ears. I don't want him hearing this. He's very sensitive."

Sabrina did her best, though the dog squirmed in her arms and licked every inch of her face.

"OK, big guy," Beauty said to Canis. "Let's go back in time. I want you to go to the night you met Little Red Riding Hood. Are you there?"

"Yes."

"Good. Tell me what you see and hear."

Canis shook his head. "It's fuzzy. I can't make out anything."

"Concentrate," Beauty said. "Push through the fuzziness. Try to bring the scene into focus."

Canis's body tightened. His head swung back and forth violently.

"He's fighting me," Beauty told the group.

"Keep trying," Little John pressed as he anxiously watched the door for Nottingham's return.

"It doesn't work like that," Beauty snapped. "It's not a matter of trying harder. His mind either opens up or it doesn't. There's something he doesn't want to tell me."

Suddenly, Canis relaxed. "I'm running."

"Where to?" Beauty asked.

"There's a tiny house in the woods."

"Can you see anything else?" Beauty asked.

"Light, so much light. It's blinding me, and the trees are leaning over," he said.

"He's talking crazy like Red," Sabrina whispered to her grandmother.

"Why are the trees leaning over?" Beauty asked.

Canis shook his head. "The wind is incredible. I'm pounding on the door. I want him to follow me. I need his help, but . . ."

"Who are you talking about, Mr. Canis? Is there someone with you?" Beauty asked.

Canis ignored her. "I'm inside the house. The old woman is there. The child is crying."

"Are you talking about Red Riding Hood?" Beauty asked.

Canis nodded. "Yes. There is so much wind."

"Inside the house?" Beauty turned to the lawyers, her brow furrowed. "Is any of this making sense to you?"

Robin shrugged. "Ask him if he sees any cages."

Beauty repeated the question, and for a long moment the old man was silent. Then he nodded. "Yes, cages," he said. "Something is locked in one of them, but the wind is so strong, I can't see it. It's some kind of animal. It's loose! It's coming at me!" Canis let out a horrible scream that startled everyone. Then his eyes flickered open, and he stared at Beauty. "Who's that playing around in my head?"

The princess leaped up and scurried toward the cell door. Luckily, the chains that bound the Wolf's arms and legs held him in place as he lunged forward. Though restrained, he laughed at Beauty's terror and promised to kill her as soon as he got the chance. Then he turned to the Grimm family with a sinister smile. "Your day is coming, too."

After Little John locked the cell door once more, Canis seemed to regain control of himself. He apologized and slumped back into his corner.

"I'm not going back in there," Beauty gasped, struggling to catch her breath. "Not even my soon-to-be ex-husband was this difficult."

"You and Beast are splitting up?" Robin said with a sly grin.

"Does your wife, Marian, know what a flirt you are?" Beauty asked with a little laugh.

"Beauty, I'm terribly sorry. The two of you have been together for centuries," Granny said.

"He's run off to join the Scarlet Hand, and I can't convince him to give it up. I just can't reach him anymore. Beast thinks Everafters should be in charge. He believes the Master is going to rule the world, and we'll enslave the human race, blah, blah, blah . . . I remember the last time this nonsense came up. That's how we all got trapped in this town in the first place. I'll have none of it. All I want from this world is a new pair of shoes for every day of the year."

The dog let out a yelp.

Beauty reached over to Sabrina and took her dog. "And, of course, a diamond-studded collar for Mr. Wuggles," she cooed, showering the slobbery little mutt with kisses. He licked her face happily.

"The only thing you're going to get is the edge of my blade, you traitorous idiot," a voice bellowed from the doorway. The group spun around to see Nottingham step into the room, wielding his dagger.

The North Wind

6

NOTTINGHAM CHARGED TOWARD BEAUTY BUT met Little John's fist instead. He fell against the bars of the jail cell but rebounded quickly. Chaos erupted—flying fists and slashing daggers—with the girls caught in the center. Sabrina grabbed Daphne by the arm, and they dodged out of the fight until they could join their grandmother, Beauty, and Mr. Wuggles huddled in a corner. Moments later, the lawyers had subdued the sheriff, though he continued to kick and curse.

"You're all going to find yourselves at the end of a hangman's noose, just like your mongrel friend," Nottingham threatened.

"What should we do with him?" Little John asked his colleague.

Robin shrugged. "I haven't the foggiest."

"He'll tell everyone I was helping you," Beauty cried. "The

Scarlet Hand will come after me. It won't matter if my husband is a member."

"I'm afraid she's right, Robin," Granny said. "Beauty won't be safe."

"Princess, have you ever done your little hypno trick on a person?" Robin asked.

"It only works on wild beasts."

"Well, he's about as wild a beast as a man can get," Little John said. "It couldn't hurt to try, could it?"

Beauty shrugged, then knelt to place her hand on Nottingham's forehead. He fought with all his strength, but it was no use. All the fight quickly seeped out of him, and he turned as docile as a turtle.

"Go to sleep," Beauty instructed, and the sheriff did as he was told, closing his eyes and falling into a deep, peaceful slumber. "Sheriff, you're not going to remember the fight that just happened. You aren't going to remember you found us in your jail. You aren't going to remember me or anyone who was here."

"I won't?" the sheriff mumbled dreamily.

"No, you won't."

"OK."

"Wow," Sabrina said.

Robin Hood stared in awe. "Beauty, you never cease to amaze me. Now that we have crankypants under control, I wonder if we could have a little fun. Can you plant a secret message in his mind? I once saw a hypnotist do it during a magic show. Every time he said a certain word, his volunteer would cluck like a chicken."

Little John grinned. "You're a genius."

Beauty laughed mischievously. "I suppose I could, but . . . what do you think, Mr. Wuggles?"

The dog barked.

"Let's do it. What exactly do you have in mind, Mr. Hood?" the princess asked.

Sabrina was certain it had been the longest day of her life. When she finally kicked off her shoes, she found blisters on top of her blisters. Daphne practically fell asleep standing up. And Granny Relda, who usually possessed more energy than both girls combined, melted into a chair, propping her legs up on an ottoman. Elvis trotted down the stairs and delivered sympathetic kisses to each of the exhausted Grimms.

"Elvis, will you give me a ride to bed?" Daphne asked. "I think I'm too tired to climb the steps."

"Long day? I'm afraid I don't have any good news," Uncle Jake said, coming downstairs from Mirror's room. He explained that Goldilocks had hopped a flight out of Venice after the incident with the motorcyclist, and he'd totally lost track of her. They would have to wait until she landed to make their next move.

Sabrina was disappointed. Keeping an eye on their elusive heroine would have been a nice distraction from the horrible image that played over and over in her mind. Mr. Canis—no, the Wolf—was roaring for her attention.

The memory of the Wolf's face when he suddenly took charge of Canis's body kept her awake most of the night. He'd promised to kill her family as soon as he got the chance. His wicked, smiling eyes floated in her imagination. She wished she could talk to someone about her fears, but every time she mentioned the old man to the rest of the family, they got so defensive that they stopped listening to her. It was as if they refused to see what Mr. Canis was becoming.

The Wolf's threats didn't seem to bother her little sister. Daphne was so trusting, so naïve. Tucked in bed next to her, the little girl slept soundly, unafraid. Sabrina knew there was nothing she could do by herself to stop him, unless . . .

She sat up in bed and looked at her sister. The chain around Daphne's neck held the key that unlocked the safe-deposit box storing the weapon the Three Pigs swore could save them all. Why had Mr. Hamstead entrusted such a huge responsibility to such a little girl? Sure, Daphne had a talent for enchanted items, and Sabrina—well, she and magic didn't mix. But regardless of what the weapon was made of, it had to be used by someone who saw things clearly, someone who could put sentimentality aside to fight for her family. And who knew the possibilities? Maybe the weapon could put Mr. Canis back in control of himself. Or, if the family had it, things might get easier for them in Ferryport Landing. They could use it to fight the Scarlet Hand. It was long past time to go find the mysterious weapon. Daphne was just being stubborn. Luckily, she had her big sister, who knew what had to be done.

Sabrina leaned over and gently unfastened the chain from Daphne's neck. The little girl was such a deep sleeper, she didn't notice it was gone. When it was safely in her hands, Sabrina studied it, imagining what might lie within the box it opened. Then, she gingerly crawled out of bed and padded down the hallway to Mirror's room. When Sabrina stepped inside, Mirror's horrifying face suddenly appeared in the reflection, accompanied by frightening bolts of lightning.

"Who dares invade my sanctuary?" Mirror bellowed.

"Shhhh!" Sabrina begged. "You'll wake the whole house. It's just me!"

The threatening image faded, replaced by the kind face of her friend. "Up a little late, aren't you, Sabrina?"

"I'm on a secret mission," Sabrina replied.

"Is this mission secret from your grandmother?"

Sabrina nodded, then turned her attention to the traveler's chest. She bent over to lift the lid, but it was locked tight. Uncle Jake had the only key, and there was no way he was going to give her permission to retrieve such a dangerous weapon. Plus, he was firmly on Mr. Canis's side. She'd have to go with plan B, even if it nauseated her. "I need the flying carpet."

"What for?"

"I can't tell you," she said.

"I'm not surprised." Mirror rolled his eyes. "Still, where's your sister? Where's Puck? You never go alone."

"This time I don't have a choice," Sabrina said, holding out her set of keys to the Hall of Wonders.

"I don't know about this, kiddo," Mirror said.

"I won't be gone long, I promise. And later, you'll see that what I'm doing is for everyone's good."

"I suppose there's no stopping you. I swear, if I still had hair, you would turn it gray," he said, taking the keys and disappearing from view. Moments later, he returned with the rug. "Would you listen if I asked you to be careful?"

Sabrina nodded as she opened the room's window. "I always listen to you."

"Yes, but do you hear me?"

She gave him a wink and unrolled the rug, admiring the beautifully embroidered stars, moons, and sabers woven into it by hand.

She sat down in the center and clutched its tassels tightly. Then she took a deep breath to calm her nerves. She hated the flying carpet.

"OK, carpet, take me to the Ferryport Landing National Bank," she commanded.

"What's at the bank?" Mirror asked.

"The answer to a lot of our problems," Sabrina replied as the rug rose off the ground and darted out the window. Sabrina hung on for dear life. She flew over the forest, the air whipping through her hair. To take her mind off the dizzying height, Sabrina contemplated the weapon she was after. Swineheart and Boarman promised it was powerful. Perhaps it was a bazooka, or a laser gun, or a cannon that shot lava. It didn't really matter to her. If it had helped three out-of-shape piggies beat a raging monster, it was exactly what the Grimms needed.

The carpet descended the moment Sabrina caught sight of the bank, landing gently on the deserted sidewalk in front of the building. Sabrina scanned the street, confirming that no one was watching. The carpet rolled itself up, and Sabrina stashed it behind a nearby bush. The coast clear, she approached the front door and found a sign that read CLOSED.

Sabrina could have kicked herself for being so stupid. Of course, the bank was closed—it was the middle of the night! Her eagerness had kept her from thinking clearly. What was she going to do now? She couldn't come back later. Her family was always around, and Daphne would notice her key missing. She sat down on the stoop, hopeless, when a crazy idea popped into her head. Why not break into the bank? She and her sister had done much crazier things since moving to Ferryport Landing. She just needed to break a window and crawl inside.

She turned and sized up building the same way she used to size up each new foster home Ms. Smirt forced her and Daphne into. Each one had a weakness, and Sabrina had a knack for spotting them—it was how the girls had escaped from so many weirdos.

She recalled the Deasy family, who owned and operated an ostrich farm in Hoboken, New Jersey. The gigantic, flightless birds were frightening, chasing the sisters nearly nonstop for the first three days. When one of them spat in Sabrina's face, she knew it was time to go. Sabrina picked the lock on the front gate, freeing herself, Daphne, and the entire herd of giant, stinky birds. She and her sister hopped the turnstile to board the underground train that led to New York City. They were back in the Big Apple hours before the Hoboken Police Department managed to track and capture even one of the twenty-five angry ostriches. Sabrina was a pro at escaping, so how hard could breaking in be?

She searched the street for a sharp stone and found one heavy enough to crack the bank's thick security windows. She found the perfect place to fling it, spotting a window low to the ground at the back of the building. She peeked inside and spotted wires attached to the window that led to a bright red bell on the wall: the alarm. Breaking the window would surely set off the alarm, so she'd have to act fast. She needed to open the safe-deposit box, grab the weapon, and escape before Nottingham arrived.

She closed her eyes, said a silent prayer, then reared back and threw. The rock should have smashed against the window, shattering the glass and setting off the alarm. But none of those things happened. Instead, she heard a voice.

"Sabrina Grimm turns to a life of crime. I'm so proud of you." Puck was hovering above her with her rock firmly in his hand.

"What are you doing here?" Sabrina demanded, dragging him down to the ground and into the shadows.

"Keeping an eye on you," Puck said. "You slipped past all my security. You know, you truly are an ungrateful jerk. Do you know how much money I have to pay the troglodyte to sit inside the laundry hamper? Not to mention the brownies living in the bushes outside and the ogre under the couch. Professional bodyguards are not cheap. Plus, I have to pay their dental insurance and contribute to their 401(k) plans. But do you appreciate it? NO! You run around this town willy-nilly, flaunting your face at danger. Well, listen, bub, if you and your family get killed, then I'm out in the cold. That means no more free meals. No more cable TV. Do you know what would happen to me if I had to go back down to just three or four channels?" Puck shuddered.

Sabrina rolled her eyes.

"So let's get something clear. From now on you need to check in with your bodyguards before you sneak out."

"I can't sneak out if someone knows I'm sneaking out," Sabrina argued. "That takes the sneak out of the sneaking out! Besides, you're taking this whole security thing too far. I don't need bodyguards. I can handle myself just fine."

"Like you handled the giant? And the spider boy? And the fifty-foot wicked witch robot?" Puck huffed. "Are you saying you're not going to cooperate?"

"Now you get it."

"I suppose I should just give up, then, huh? I guess you've won . . ." Puck grinned.

"Listen, I'm busy. Give me the rock and go home."

"Why do you want the rock?"

"I'm trying to break that window."

"Hey, I understand the urge to break things," Puck said. "If I don't smash a window four or five times a day, I don't feel like myself. Still, it doesn't seem like your style."

"I'm not breaking windows just to break windows. I need to get into the bank. There's something inside I have to get," Sabrina said.

"That's what all the bank robbers say."

"I'm not robbing the bank!"

"Then what are you going to steal? They chain the pens to the counters, you know."

"I'm not stealing anything. I'm breaking in to get something that belongs to us. I just can't wait for the bank to open."

"Sabrina Grimm! I'm impressed. I'll help."

Sabrina felt like telling Puck to get lost, but she realized the fairy boy had skills that could come in handy.

"Fine, but—" Sabrina said.

Puck grinned and tossed the rock aside. "I've never been one to suggest breaking a window is wrong, but sometimes there are easier ways to get things done." He pulled a small wooden flute from his pocket and blasted a few notes into the air. Moments later, a throng of little lights circled them. They were pixies, and they obeyed Puck's every command. The boy raised his hands, and all the lights stopped in midair.

"Minions," he said, "we need to get into this bank."

The pixies twittered with excitement, then circled the building as if looking for a crack or crevice to invade. They discovered an opening, and soon Sabrina spotted a few pixies flying around inside the bank. Sabrina and Puck rushed to the front door just as it swept open. They hurried inside, and Sabrina hoped no one saw the peculiar break-in.

"I believe the words you're looking for are *thank you*," Puck said as he returned his flute to his pocket.

"Thank you," Sabrina said, rolling her eyes. "Now, we've got to act fast. We might have tripped a silent alarm, so Nottingham could be on his way."

"What are we looking for, anyway?"

"We need to find the room where they keep the safe-deposit boxes."

Puck repeated the instructions to the pixies, and they flew off in different directions to search. Sabrina didn't wait for them to return. She went searching on her own, opening one door after another. But each room was a dead end, and each dead end made her more and more anxious that Nottingham would arrive at any moment.

Luckily, Puck eventually found the room himself. She heard him calling from the other side of the bank and raced to join him. She found him hovering in a room lined with hundreds of little silver doors and one enormous round vault door. Sabrina studied the silver doors carefully. Each had a number carved above a keyhole. She found the number engraved on her key; it read TH192.

"What's the big deal about this safe-deposit box?" Puck asked as he marveled at all the doors.

"It has a weapon inside it."

"What kind of weapon?" Puck asked, raising his eyebrows.

Sabrina shrugged. "Before we left New York City, Sheriff Hamstead gave Daphne this key and told her it unlocked a powerful weapon. He said to get it if Mr. Canis lost control of the Wolf. It's the only thing that can truly stop him."

"If he gave it to Daphne, then how come you have it?" Puck asked.

Sabrina lowered her eyes. "She doesn't understand."

"You stole it?"

"Is the Trickster King going to give me a lecture on being a good person? I'm doing this to protect everyone," Sabrina argued. "This weapon could help us fight the Scarlet Hand, too."

Puck said nothing; he didn't have to. Sabrina could sense his disapproval, though it boggled her mind. Who was Puck to tell her how to behave?

"There it is," he said, pointing to a slot in the wall.

Sabrina checked the number on the drawer—it matched the one on the key. She slipped it into the slot, turned it, and felt the latch click open. She pulled out the drawer, her mind swirling with possibilities. She opened the lid and found a small blue velvet bag tied with a string. The words THE NORTH WIND were stitched into the fabric in gold thread. Sabrina picked it up, surprised by how light and delicate it felt.

"What is it?" Puck asked.

Sabrina ignored him, opening the bag to peer inside it. She expected to find a magical amulet, maybe one that shot energy, or perhaps a powerful wand; but instead, much to her chagrin, she found a kazoo.

"It's a toy," Sabrina said.

Puck pulled the kazoo from the sack and waved it in Sabrina's face. "This is your secret weapon?"

Sabrina was too crushed to speak. She felt as if someone had punched her in the gut. All of her hopes had just vanished, replaced by someone's idea of a twisted joke. She stormed out of the room and out the front door of the bank.

"Hey! What's wrong with you?" Puck asked, chasing after her.

"We're doomed!"

"No, you're not," Puck said. "I'll protect you."

"Yeah, like I can rely on an immature fairy whose biggest enemy is a bar of soap?"

Her words seemed to sting the boy, and she expected a torrent of insults in retaliation, but instead he just looked down at the kazoo.

"Maybe there's something more to this thing. How does it work?"

"It's a toy instrument, Puck," she said. "You blow into it."

He blew into it, but only a whistle of air escaped.

"Is it broken?" he asked.

Frustrated, Sabrina snatched the kazoo and put it into her mouth. She knew there was a trick to making the sound—a sort of hum into one end that would produce a fuzzy musical note out the other. She blew into it, but, instead of a pitchy note, she felt the familiar, uncomfortable tingle of magic. A horrible whooshing sound came out, and an intense whipping wind built into a brutal storm. Right before her eyes, the windows of the bank imploded. The roof flew off and the walls crumbled. When the violent wind finally died down, there was no evidence that a bank or any other kind of building had ever stood in that spot.

Sabrina gaped at the kazoo, speechless.

"Well, if you don't want it, I'll take it," Puck said.

7

SABRINA AND PUCK SLIPPED BACK INTO THE house without incident. He followed her into her bedroom and watched as she stuffed the magic carpet under her bed. She would return it to Mirror in the morning, but for now she didn't need another set of disapproving eyes on her. Puck's were more than enough. He watched with a frown as she carefully placed the chain with the key back around her sleeping sister's neck.

"I did what had to be done," Sabrina said as she kicked off her shoes and crawled under the blankets. "So save your lecture."

"What would be the point? I'm just giving you one last chance to reconsider the bodyguards," Puck said.

She laughed dismissively, then braced for an argument. But, much to her surprise, he turned and left the room.

Sabrina nestled into her bed. *I think that boy is finally getting some sense*, she thought.

As she drifted off to sleep, she reached into her pocket for the kazoo. She could feel the unhealthy ache of magic, but the bag seemed to dull the sensation. Still, Sabrina knew she would have to be careful. After all, she couldn't count on the others this time. She was on her own.

The next morning, Sabrina woke to the sun flooding through her bedroom window and into her face. She reached to pull her pillow over her head, but her wrist was caught on something. She sat up in bed and held her hand up to her face. A handcuff was clamped tightly around her wrist, and the other end was fastened to the wrist of a shaggy-haired boy asleep in a rocking chair next to her bed.

"PUCK!" Sabrina cried. She pulled so hard on her end of the handcuffs that he tumbled out of the chair and onto the floor. Unfortunately, the fall dragged her out of bed, as well, and she fell on top of him.

"I was in the middle of the best dream!" Puck whined, rubbing the sleep from his eyes. "I discovered a village of marshmallow people who begged me to toast and eat them. Why did you have to wake me up?"

"What is this about?" Sabrina said, shaking the handcuffs violently.

"Oh yeah. Unfortunately, you've made that necessary," Puck explained. "You wouldn't work with my staff, so from now on I'm going to be your personal bodyguard."

"This is insane," Sabrina said as she tried to pull herself free.

"Trust me, being downwind of you twenty-four hours a day is not what I call a good time, but you've left me no choice."

"Twenty-four hours a day?" Sabrina screamed. "You better have the key!"

Puck took a tiny golden key out of his pocket. "Of course I have the key, and I know the perfect place to keep it safe."

Puck popped the key into his mouth and swallowed dramatically. Sabrina shrieked.

"Are you deranged?" she yelled as she climbed to her feet and stormed downstairs, dragging Puck behind her.

Granny Relda was no help. In fact, she, Uncle Jake, and Daphne found the whole situation hilarious. They snickered all through breakfast.

"Sabrina, Puck is just trying to help," Granny said. "Perhaps you do need a little personal attention. There's not much I can do about it, anyway. If he swallowed the key, all we can do is wait."

"Wait for what?" Daphne asked, but then the answer must have to come to her because she turned green and groaned.

"I wouldn't hold your breath on that one," Puck said, scooping a handful of oatmeal into his mouth.

"How am I going to get dressed? Or take a bath?" Sabrina cried.

"Who needs a bath?" Puck said, wiping the extra oatmeal on his shirt.

"I suppose we could just take the two of you out in the yard and hose you down," Uncle Jake said.

"Yeah, Elvis loves it," Daphne added.

Uncle Jake laughed so hard, his scrambled eggs fell out of his mouth.

Daphne finished her breakfast, and for the first time ever, Sabrina watched the little girl push her empty plate away without asking for seconds. Sabrina guessed this latest quirk had something to do with Daphne's new "grown-up" attitude. Daphne was wearing more of Sabrina's clothes and a pair of high-heel shoes she'd found in Granny's closet.

"I had a thought about Mr. Canis's case last night," Daphne announced.

"Oh?" Granny said.

"There are so many versions of the Red Riding Hood story. A few of them have a woodcutter who rescues her from the Wolf. Has anyone talked to him?"

Granny's eyes lit up. "*Liebling*, that's brilliant detective work. He might be able to give us his account of that day."

"But who is he?" Uncle Jake asked. "I'm not sure he's even in Ferryport Landing. A lot of Everafters decided to stay in the old country instead of coming to America."

Granny clapped her hands and rushed to the family journals. "There's only one way to find out."

"I'll help," Daphne sang eagerly.

Granny grinned and handed her a book. "What about you, Sabrina?"

She nodded, though she didn't feel entirely honest. Even with the magic kazoo in her pocket, she worried what might happen if Mr. Canis was freed. Still, she needed to get back into the family's good graces, especially her grandmother's, so she snatched up a copy of *The Complete Fairy Tales of Charles Perrault*, forcing a protesting Puck along with her.

Perrault's book was published in 1697, long before the Brothers Grimm put pen to paper. He was one of the original fairy-tale detectives, and his account of Red Riding Hood included a woodcutter who came to her rescue. Sabrina was impressed with the woodcutter's heroics. Not too many who faced the Wolf lived to tell the tale.

Sabrina noted the story and continued her research, this time digging into the sizable collection of family journals. Each contained detailed descriptions of Everafter activities in Ferryport Landing. Sabrina and Daphne had filled a couple themselves during their short time in town.

Sabrina scanned hundreds of entries. She read about a failed military coup against the mouse king. She found sheet music composed by Little Boy Blue. She learned that the Three Blind Mice had once applied for seeing-eye dogs. But she didn't find anything on a woodcutter or where he might be.

She closed the last of her share of the journals and sat back in defeat. "I've got nothing."

Granny sighed. "I didn't find anything, either."

"Perhaps we should just ask Mirror," Uncle Jake suggested. "He found Goldilocks easily enough."

Daphne looked up from her book. "What does the word *mani . . . mani . . . fest* mean?"

"You mean *manifest*? It's a list of items on a train, bus, truck, or ship," Granny explained.

"Where's your dictionary?" Sabrina mocked.

Daphne stuck her tongue out but otherwise ignored her sister's question. "Can it be a list of people, too?"

"Sure," the old woman said. "What did you find?"

"This," the little girl said, handing a journal to her grandmother. "It looks like a list of the passengers on the *New Beginning*."

Sabrina leaned over to take a look. The *New Beginning* was the name of the boat Jacob and Wilhelm Grimm had used to transport Everafter immigrants to New York.

"Good work, Daphne. Let's see if there's a woodcutter here." Granny perused the list. "Hmm, I'm not seeing one. If only we knew his name."

Jacob shook his head. "We don't need to know his name. We already know the names of almost everyone else on the ship. Just find the ones you don't recognize."

"Is this going to take long? I have plans," Puck grumbled.

"The handcuffs were your idea, buster. Any chance we're going to see that key pop up soon?" Sabrina said.

Puck shook his head.

The family went through the list one by one, checking off everyone they knew by name. There were quite a number of Everafters in Ferryport Landing who went by their titles rather than their real names: the Mad Hatter, the Beast, the Sheriff of Nottingham, and the Queen of Hearts, for example. It made the search much easier. Soon, they had narrowed down the list to only twenty citizens none of them could identify. Seven of them had odd, almost unpronounceable names. Granny guessed they were witches, goblins, or trolls. Eight more were obviously animals, including Hans the Hedgehog and someone called the Sawhorse. That left five names, and two of those were female. The story clearly suggested that the woodcutter was a man.

The phone rang, and Granny answered. "Little John! We've been trying to track down another eyewitness. We believe the woodcutter might actually live in Ferryport Landing. What's that?" She paused. "Oh dear, of course. We're on our way."

"What's going on?" Uncle Jake asked when his mother hung up.

"They're starting the trial early today, and Bluebeard has a new witness. We have to go over there right now!"

"Who's the witness?" Daphne asked.

"His name is Howard Hatchett," Granny replied.

Sabrina cringed. "Howard Hatchett is on this list."

The group drove up and down Main Street looking for a parking space. Granny commented that she had never seen downtown Ferryport Landing so busy, even when there were other humans living in town. While they searched, they passed the site where the bank had once stood.

"I've heard of people robbing banks, but I've never heard of anyone stealing the bank itself," Uncle Jake said, peering at the vacant lot.

"That's quite peculiar," Granny said. Sabrina listened for a hint that the old woman knew the truth about the bank, but she seemed just as shocked as everyone else.

Daphne poked her head out the car window, craning her neck for a better view. She turned to Sabrina with a panicked expression. "What happened?" she mouthed.

Sabrina shrugged, though her heart burned with her betrayal. Stealing from her sister was bad enough, but now that she had added lying to her list of crimes, Daphne believed their secret weapon was lost. From the look on Puck's face, Sabrina could tell he wanted her to be honest, but she wasn't sure how to explain her actions in a way that Daphne would understand.

Uncle Jake finally parked the car, and the family rushed into the courtroom before the card guards could slam the doors in their faces. Once inside, Daphne pulled her sister aside.

"OK, I was wrong," she said in a whisper. Her face was red, and tears were swimming in her eyes. "I was being stubborn. I should have let you get the weapon while we had the chance. Now it's gone."

"Yes, well, you wanted to be in charge, and—"

Puck kicked Sabrina in the leg and shot her an angry look.

"What are we going to do if we need it?" Daphne cried.

"Don't worry. I have a feeling it will turn up."

Granny snatched the girls by the sleeves. "Come along, *lieblings*. The trial is starting."

The courtroom was a standing-room-only affair, and curious Everafters were jostling for the best views. News of the case had spread, and it seemed as if the whole town had come to see what everyone was calling "the trial of every century."

Sabrina watched Mayor Heart and Sheriff Nottingham gaze at the crowd with delight. Heart commented to Nottingham they should have sold tickets. They both broke into wicked laughter.

Several of the Grimms' friends were there to offer support. Gepetto had closed his toy shop to come and be by the family's side. Cinderella and her human husband, Tom, offered to bring by dinner later. Mr. Seven sat on a stack of phone books in the back row and flashed them "thumbs-up" gestures. Even Briar Rose's fairy godmothers wished them well. But most surprising was Snow White, who sat down next to Granny Relda. She said nothing. Instead, she took the old woman's hand in her own and held it tightly.

"I'm sorry, Snow," the old woman said. "William made me promise to keep his secret."

Ms. White nodded. "I understand you were in a difficult situation. Honestly, I wish I had never found him."

Sabrina spotted the former mayor sitting stoically in the jury box, avoiding their eyes.

Briar Rose joined the group, nestling next to Uncle Jake. When she took his hand, Uncle Jake smiled. "Thank you for being here."

"Where else would I be?" she asked.

"Are you sure you want the whole town knowing you're dating a Grimm?"

Briar kissed him on the cheek. "I'm not worried about the whole town. If I can keep my fairy godmothers from turning you into a toad, we'll be just fine," she said, giggling.

There was light in their eyes and laughter in their voices, and they couldn't seem to hold each other tightly enough. Sabrina had seen the same behavior in her parents. It was happening fast, almost like it happened in fairy-tale stories—the sleepy princess and her swashbuckling uncle were falling madly in love.

Robin Hood and Little John entered the courtroom just as several card guards led Mr. Canis to his seat. Their old friend looked even more tired and ragged than he had the day before. Robin patted the old man reassuringly on the shoulder, and then he turned to watch Bluebeard. The villain bent down to speak to Ms. White, bringing his face close to hers.

"Snow, someone should arrest you. It has to be a crime to be so beautiful," he said.

Snow gave a forced smile, but when the creepy man turned away, Sabrina caught her grimace as if there were a bitter taste in her mouth. Daphne, who'd witnessed the exchange, had the same look on her face.

"All rise!" the Three of Spades shouted. "The Honorable Judge Hatter is now presiding."

Hatter stumbled in carrying a sledgehammer on his shoulder and tripping over his long black robes. When he got to his seat, he looked around the courtroom as if he wasn't quite sure where he was.

"Oh, you're back. Well, I suppose we should start the trial," he said. He slammed his sledgehammer down on the desk with a crash, causing the wood to explode into splinters. "Mr. Bluebeard, do you have another witness?"

"Indeed, I do! The prosecution calls Howard Hatchett to the stand."

The double doors opened and a man in a flashy blue suit entered. He had a bushy red beard and a veiny, bulbous nose. His bright red ball cap advertised something called Hatchettland.

He looked around the courtroom and jumped when he saw Mr. Canis. Two card guards stopped him from running back through the doors and forced him onto the witness stand.

Bluebeard thanked him for taking the time to testify, but Hatchett didn't seem to hear him. His eyes were locked on Mr. Canis.

"Mr. Hatchett, are you well?" Bluebeard asked.

"I'm . . . I'm fine," Hatchett said, shifting in his seat. "I have to admit, I never thought I'd see this day."

"Mr. Hatchett, could you tell the jury who you are?" Bluebeard asked.

"M—my name is Howard Hatchett," he stammered. "I'm an Everafter."

Sabrina watched Canis frown.

"Mr. Hatchett, have you ever heard the story of Red Riding Hood?"

"Heard it? I'm in it! I was the one who saved her from the Wolf."

There was a murmur in the crowd, but when the judge lifted his sledgehammer, the room fell silent.

"Are you saying you were there the day Red Riding Hood's grandmother was killed?"

Hatchett nodded, keeping his eyes on Canis.

"Please respond verbally, Mr. Hatchett."

"Y—yes," he croaked.

"What kind of work do you do, Mr. Hatchett?"

"Well, I . . . I used to be a woodcutter. I cut down trees and sold the lumber to mills. I started out working for a man, but then I went into business for myself," Hatchett said, still watching Canis. "Then one day I thought to myself, 'Hey! I'm one of literature's greatest heroes!'"

"What did he say?" Daphne whispered.

"He's bragging," Puck replied.

"I saved Little Red Riding Hood's life. I faced the Big Bad Wolf and lived to tell the tale. I'm an idol to millions." He counted off his heroics on his fingers. "I realized I might as well cash in on my fame, so I started Hatchett Industries, a company dedicated to providing products to people who want to be more like me."

"Please explain," Bluebeard pressed.

"I'm their hero. People want to be like their heroes, so I sell things with my face and name on them. For instance, my Woodcutter Three-Bean Chili, Woodcutter Beef Jerky, Woodcutter Tires, Woodcutter Diaper Rash Powder, and a chain of Woodcutter Home-Cooking Restaurants. The list goes on and on."

"That's very clever," Bluebeard said.

"I agree. I've also been constructing an amusement park right here in Ferryport Landing. Our grand opening is this week."

Sabrina turned to her grandmother. "What amusement park?"

Granny shrugged. "This is the first I'm hearing about it."

"So, you're a great businessman," the lawyer said. "Perhaps you can tell us more specifically about the heroics of the day in question."

Hatchett glanced at Canis one last time, then puffed up his chest with pride. "Well, I was just a regular working stiff back then, you know, just like everybody. I never thought of myself as a hero, but there are those who stand by and watch, and there are the rare, brave few who become heroes. So, with nothing more than my wits and my ax, I raced off to help."

"What did you find?" Bluebeard asked, rapt.

"I came upon a little house in the woods. I peered through the window and saw a monster attacking a child. Well, I suppose an ordinary person might have just run away, but I'm not ordinary. People were in trouble, and I knew I would fight to the death to save them."

"You say you saw a monster. Do you see that monster in the courtroom today?"

Hatchett looked over at Canis, and for a moment, the man's flashy confidence dissolved. He pointed with a trembling hand at the old man. "It was him."

"Let the record show that Mr. Hatchett is referring to Mr. Canis," Bluebeard said, then turned his attention back to his witness. "Were you afraid?"

Hatchett shook his head. "I look back on it now and laugh. I should have been afraid, but when you're a man like me, you go to a place where fear doesn't follow."

"Oh, brother," Puck said, rolling his eyes.

The crowd turned to glare at him.

"What happened next?" Bluebeard continued.

"I pounded on the door so hard, it flew off its hinges. I'm a strong guy. I work out. I can bench about two-fifty," Hatchett bragged. "Then I rushed in with my ax raised. The Wolf had already finished off the old woman—there was nothing I could do for her, but the little girl was still in danger. Now the monster knew he didn't want to go head-to-head with me, so in desperation he swallowed the child whole."

Mr. Canis shifted uncomfortably.

"Good heavens!" Bluebeard cried. "What did you do?"

"My instincts took over. I swung my ax at the monster's belly. It split from end to end, and the little girl spilled out, perfectly healthy. I filled the Wolf's belly full of rocks and sewed it shut with some thread I found. Then, I carried his body on my back to the river and tossed him in. The weight of the rocks caused him to sink to the bottom."

"Yet he lived," Bluebeard said, gesturing at Canis.

"He's a tough customer," Hatchett replied. "But I'm tougher."

"I appreciate your time," Bluebeard replied, taking his seat. "I'm finished with this witness," he announced to the court.

Hatchett barely noticed. He continued promoting himself. "I tell the whole story at my new theme park, Hatchettland. It has rides and attractions, and it's a great place to buy my various products, including my twelve-inch Woodcutter Action Figure with Kung-Fu Grip, Woodcutter All-Protein Organic Cereal Bars, Woodcutter Toilet Paper, Woodcutter Nasal Spray, and the new six-patty Woodcutter EZ-Grill. It seals in the juices and drains the fat for perfect burgers every time!"

Robin Hood leaped to his feet. "I have some questions for you!" he shouted as he approached the witness stand.

"Order!" the judge cried, but Robin ignored him.

"You claimed you saw a monster attack the girl—can you be sure it was the Wolf?"

"Order!"

"How did you carry his huge body filled with stones over your shoulder and dump it in the river? How far away was this river? Did anyone see you do this?"

"Order! Order! Order!" the judge shrieked.

"The defense has the right to question witnesses, Your Honor!" Robin shouted.

"Objection!" Bluebeard cried.

Hatter slammed the sledgehammer down on his desk, which split into two and collapsed. "Now look what you've made me do!"

"This trial is a sham!" Little John bellowed.

"Guards, remove these men from my courtroom!" the judge

demanded. A mob of card guards rushed forward, but Robin Hood and Little John didn't go quietly. They fought and shouted that there was no justice in Ferryport Landing.

When they were gone, Judge Hatter announced, "We'll see you all here tomorrow." He darted out of the courtroom, leaving the bewildered crowd behind.

The Grimms and their friends found Robin Hood and Little John crawling out of the gutter and dusting off their clothes. Sabrina expected the men to be furious, but they were both laughing.

"It's been a while since we've been thrown out of someplace, hasn't it, old friend?" Robin said.

Little John laughed. "McSorley threw us out of his pub just last week, Robin."

"Oh, yeah, I forgot!" The men roared with laughter.

"You two seem to be in a good mood," Granny said.

"Actually, we're in a rotten mood," Little John replied. "But it's important to laugh from time to time. Especially since this case is a joke. Relda, they aren't letting us defend Canis."

"Our approach now is to cause as much of a disturbance as possible," Robin Hood said.

"I'd like to help with that," Puck offered.

"You'll get your chance soon enough, Trickster King," Robin said.

"What do you have in mind?" Uncle Jake asked.

"I think I'd like to take a visit to Mr. Hatchett's amusement park," Robin said. "I have a feeling there's more to his story than he's telling."

"You think he was lying?" Daphne asked.

"That scrawny little man couldn't carry a sack of groceries on his back, let alone the Big Bad Wolf," Little John replied. "If only we could let Canis out, I have a feeling he could get Hatchett to confess a few things he'd rather keep secret."

"We don't need the Wolf for that," Daphne said. "Can we stop at home for a second before we go see Hatchett?"

"Sure, *liebling*," Granny said. "What do you need?"

"I smell mischief," Puck said with a grin.

Granny and Daphne rushed into the house while Sabrina waited in the car with Puck. He sat quietly next to her. She could feel his disapproval in the air but was too tired to talk about it. Luckily, her grandmother and sister returned quickly with a fairy godmother wand and a risky plan.

Puck was ecstatic. "It's been a long time since I had the opportunity to pull a good prank."

"You filled my pillow with horse manure four days ago," Daphne reminded him.

"Four days is a long time," he countered.

Robin Hood and Little John pulled up outside the house and honked the car horn.

"We found an address for the amusement park," Robin said, handing Uncle Jake a slip of paper.

Jake made sure the lawyers were right behind him, then led the small caravan through the country roads of Ferryport Landing.

"Why don't we know anything about an amusement park in this town dedicated to the Red Riding Hood story?" Uncle Jake asked.

Granny shrugged and studied the address Robin Hood had given them. "He's built it on the grounds of Dr. Dolittle's old petting zoo. It went bankrupt when the animals went on strike."

"You mean that abandoned lot up on Mount Taurus?" Uncle Jake said. "That's a lousy place to put an amusement park. Who wants to ride a Ferris wheel next to a burnt-out mental hospital?"

Sabrina shuddered. It seemed as if everything about Red Riding Hood led back to Mount Taurus, including the insane asylum she'd once called home.

The amusement park looked more like a shrine to Howard Hatchett than anything else. A twenty-five-foot-tall statue of Hatchett himself greeted them at the front entrance. To get to the parking lot, they had to drive between the statue's legs. In the parking lot, they found a dozen more statues of Hatchett, including one where he stood triumphantly over a cowering wolf.

"This guy sure does love himself," Little John commented as everyone stepped out of the cars.

"He's the idol of millions, remember?" Sabrina said sarcastically.

"How do we get in?" Puck asked. "I could use some cotton candy."

"Me, too!" Daphne exclaimed.

Uncle Jake pointed to a path. A sign above it read: THIS WAY TO THE SCENE OF THE CRIME.

The group followed the path until they came to a gate with several turnstile entrances. To the right was a store called the Big Bad Gift Shop. Sabrina led everyone inside. Her entrance caused a mechanical wolf's howl to erupt from a speaker mounted above the door. A pimply-faced teenager wearing a hat with wolf ears on it put down his handheld video game and addressed the group.

"Welcome to Hatchettland," he said in a well-rehearsed voice. "Are you here to visit the park or just stopping by to stock up on all our popular Woodcutter Brand products like our gourmet Woodcutter Wasabi?"

"Actually, we were hoping we could have a word with Mr. Hatchett himself," Granny said.

"He's down at the house," the teenager said.

"The house?" Sabrina asked.

"It's at the end of the path. If you want to see him, you have to buy tickets."

The old woman sighed but purchased enough tickets to get

everyone into the park. Once inside, Sabrina spotted a sign that read: WHERE IT ALL HAPPENED—GRANNY'S HOUSE! An arrow indicated a path through the thick forest. As they walked, speakers mounted in the trees played spooky music and told the story of Little Red Riding Hood and Hatchett's selfless bravery. The speakers crackled loudly, giving Sabrina a major headache.

At the end of the path, there was a small wooden shack with a brick chimney. It looked old, with broken windows and vines growing up the walls to the roof. At odds with its shabby appearance was the bright, blinking neon sign above its door that read: GRANNY'S HOUSE.

"What on earth is this place?" Sabrina asked.

Hatchett came out of the house. He seemed startled to find such a large group waiting but quickly composed himself.

"Welcome to the park, everyone. We're thrilled you've come to spend the day with us. This, of course, is the famous house, the very location where the story takes place," Hatchett announced.

"You built a model of it?" Uncle Jake asked.

"No, this is the actual house. I had it shipped piece by piece to Ferryport Landing," Hatchett replied.

"Whatever for?" Granny asked.

"Do you know how many people know the story of Red Riding Hood? People read about it in every nation of the world, and a lot of them would pay a pretty penny to visit the actual place.

This is a bona fide tourist attraction and a historic site. Want to go inside?"

Sabrina wasn't sure. If the stories were true, horrible things had happened inside the little shack. It gave her chills just thinking about it, but Hatchett wouldn't take no for an answer.

Inside was a single room with a dirt floor. A crude table and a chair sat in one corner and a small bed sat in another. On the bed, a dressing gown was laid out on a tattered quilt. The fireplace was ablaze, and a cast-iron pot hung over the flames. Other than the fire, the room was dark, and the firelight cast shadows that slithered along the walls. Sabrina was completely unnerved. She thought she heard distant screams echoing around the room, and she soon realized the screams were coming from a speaker fixed to a rafter.

"Every time I come in here, it's like I'm transported to that day," Hatchett said.

"Good to know," Little John said. "'Cause we've got some questions about it."

Hatchett stiffened. "I've said all I'm going to say on that matter. If you want to know more, you can read my book, *Facing the Fangs: One Man's Journey into the Jaws of Death*. It's for sale in the gift shop."

Robin shook his head. "We don't have time to read your book. A man's life is in jeopardy."

"I'm afraid I'm a little busy at the moment, Mr. Hood,"

Hatchett said. "Our grand opening is today, and I'm expecting throngs of people to arrive at any moment."

Sabrina peered out the dingy window. There wasn't a soul in sight.

Granny smiled. "Children, would you like to get some air?"

Sabrina recognized the code the group had worked out beforehand. It was time to get down to business. Puck couldn't have been more excited. He dragged the girls out of the shack and closed the door behind him.

"Oh boy, oh boy, oh boy! This is going to be so much fun!" Puck squealed.

Daphne took a long, thin wand from her purse. It had a shiny silver star at the end. "Don't worry, this won't hurt at all."

"Will it make me strong like the Wolf?" Puck asked, hopeful.

"Sorry," Daphne said. "Fairy godmother wands don't work like that. You'll just look like him; you won't have any of his powers."

"Or his twisted desires, so don't try to eat anyone," Sabrina added.

"That's no fun," Puck whined. "I wish I could do this without a wand—boy, the trouble I could get into. I can shape shift into a wolf on my own, but old Big and Bad is his own breed. How long will this last?"

"I'm giving you ten minutes," Daphne said. "After that you'll be back to your old self, so don't goof off. We need to get him talking, and fast."

"Lay it on me, sister," Puck said.

Daphne flicked the wand and smacked Puck on the head. The boy winced. "I thought you said this wouldn't hurt!" But before he could complain any further, the transformation started. Hair sprouted from every pore. Fangs grew in his mouth. Claws popped out of his fingers and toes. He grew several inches and put on hundreds of pounds of muscle. Seconds later, he looked exactly like the Big Bad Wolf.

"Did it work?" Puck asked as he looked down at himself.

"You're the spitting image," Sabrina whispered. She was still handcuffed to Puck, and his new shape made her heart race. She had to take several deep breaths to calm down.

"All right, let's go introduce you to Hatchett," Daphne said, putting away the wand.

Puck nodded. "Wait, let me roar. He'll lose his mind if I roar." Puck let out a long, goofy howl that sounded nothing like a wolf.

"You might want to skip the roar," Sabrina said.

"Everyone's a critic," Puck complained.

The children reentered the little house. Instantly, Hatchett fell to the floor, scrambled into a corner, and screamed like a baby.

"Remember me?" Puck growled.

"How did you get out of jail?" Granny cried, though her acting left a lot to be desired.

"No jail can hold me. I'm the Big Bad Wolf. The only person meaner than me is Puck, the Trickster King," Puck said. "That kid is vicious."

Sabrina kicked him in the leg, from where she was hiding behind him. "Cool it, fairy boy," she hissed.

"What do you want from me?" Hatchett cried.

"Oh, I don't know, a leg would be nice," Puck said, attempting his goofy roar again.

"Tobias!" Hatchett said. "Get ahold of yourself. It's me, Howard!"

"Who's Tobias?" Little John asked.

"He's Tobias, Tobias Clay," Hatchett cried frantically. "He's a woodcutter. He hired me to be his apprentice. He's a good man. Please don't let him eat me!"

"Maybe if you tell us the truth, the Wolf will have some mercy," Uncle Jake added, trying to sustain the illusion.

"The truth! Yes, I'll tell the truth. Tobias and I were working in the forest collecting wood for the local mill. I had only been working for him for a few weeks, but I was already surpassing his skill."

Puck growled.

"OK! He was about to fire me. I was goofing off, taking breaks, and making Tobias do all the work. He gave me one last chance, but I didn't care," Hatchett said. "I hated cutting down trees.

"We were working in one of the dark parts of the forest when we heard a scream. Tobias wanted to go check it out, but I told him to ignore it. The woods were dangerous. It could have been anything—bandits, witches, goblins. I said we would be fools to investigate, but he wouldn't listen. So we tramped through the brush until we came upon this house. There was a horrible storm above it, like a tornado, only it hovered directly overhead. Tobias didn't care. He dragged me to the hut, and we looked inside. There was an old woman, and one look at her was all I needed to know she was a witch."

"A witch?" Robin repeated.

"That can't be!" Granny shouted.

"She was a witch, all right! She was screaming and blowing into a kazoo."

"A kazoo?" Daphne cried in disbelief. "Don't lie to us. Our friend hasn't had his lunch yet, you know."

Hatchett trembled, but he continued. "I swear, it's the truth. Each time she blew into it, a wind blasted the room, blowing everything this way and that. It was almost like she controlled the wind itself. It was all so bizarre . . . not to mention the cages. They were empty except for one—it had a rabid wolf locked inside, snarling and howling and foaming at the mouth."

"What was she doing to the wolf?" Robin asked.

"That's the thing. I really have no idea. I've never seen anything like it. It was kind of like she was using the wind to split the animal into two pieces," Hatchett explained.

"Gross!" Daphne exclaimed.

"Not physically!" Hatchett clarified. "The wind seemed to pull the madness out of the animal . . . like it was taking the wolf's dark self out, making two different wolves. The first wolf was a normal, healthy animal. The second one was made out of shadows and viciousness. The old witch trapped the shadow wolf in a clay jar and put a stopper on it. Then the wind disappeared as if it had never been there at all. And the wolf in the cage was as tame as a golden retriever."

"Get to the point!" Puck growled, baring his fangs. "We don't care about some regular wolf. When did the Big Bad . . . I mean me! When did I show up?"

"Let him finish, Wolf," Uncle Jake said.

Hatchett squealed in terror. "I begged Tobias to leave. I told him there was nothing we could do without help, but then the little girl arrived."

"Red Riding Hood?" Robin asked.

Hatchett nodded. "She came skipping up to the house with her basket of goodies and knocked on the door. The witch answered, and they hugged, and—"

"Whoa! They hugged?" Sabrina repeated.

"The witch was her grandmother; that's how she coaxed the kid into one of the cages."

"He's making this up," Uncle Jake said.

"I am not! The witch locked Red in a cage and then turned the kazoo on her, and right before my eyes I saw the little girl splitting in two, just as the wolf had. I told Tobias it was none of our business, but he wouldn't listen. He stormed into the house and attacked the witch. They wrestled and fought until Tobias knocked that clay jar out of her hand. It shattered on the ground and then—well, you wanted to know when the Wolf showed up? That's when."

"I'm confused, Howard," Granny said. "That's when what?"

"The shadow that was trapped in the jar wrapped itself around Tobias. It seeped into his pores, and my boss turned into the Big Bad Wolf."

Sabrina reached into her pocket and felt the tingling energy of the kazoo. The tiny object had big secrets, bigger than she had originally suspected.

"Red's grandmother created the Big Bad Wolf?" Daphne asked.

Hatchett nodded. "She tore whatever was in the rabid animal out, and then that went into Tobias. It changed him into a monster, and, after that, he didn't exist anymore. The Wolf was in total control. That is, until fifteen years ago, when I heard he was a man again and calling himself Canis. Now you know everything. Please, call off the beast!" he begged.

"Not so fast. What happened to the grandmother?" Sabrina asked.

"The witch fought him with magic. She cast so many spells, but none could hurt the Wolf. He just kept fighting, and she was no match for him," Hatchett said as he looked into Puck's face. "I mean, she was no match for you."

"Did you even fight the Wolf? Is any of the story true?" Uncle Jake asked.

"No," Hatchett admitted. "I hid. After a little while, when I was sure the Wolf was gone, I went back for the child. I took her back to the village, but her family had abandoned her—they had moved away. I took her to a local church and left her on the doorstep."

"How kind," Granny said bitterly.

"And ever since you've been telling lies about how you saved her," Sabrina spat, disgusted.

"I didn't think it could hurt anybody! Tobias was gone. The witch was dead. The child was out of her mind. I was the only witness."

"You took advantage of a little girl who saw her grandmother's murder," Little John snapped. "What she saw drove her insane!"

"That's not my fault," Hatchett said, then burst into tears. "She was crazy when she showed up at the house! You could see it in her face. Why do you think her parents abandoned her? Even her grandmother was afraid."

Robin tapped Puck on his huge shoulders. "Let him up."

"Aw, c'mon. He hasn't wet his pants yet," Puck said. "Oh well, I think the mojo is wearing off anyway."

With those words, Puck's disguise began to fade. Soon, he was back to a fairy boy. Hatchett was bewildered.

"What's this? You tricked me!"

"We've had to learn to play dirty, too," Robin said. "What you've told us is going to be a great help in proving Mr. Canis is an innocent man. He wasn't responsible for what happened to Red's grandmother. It was the monster she helped create."

Hatchett turned red with anger. "No one will believe you! I'll tell them you're making it all up. I'm the hero. They'll believe me."

"I'm sure you're right," Robin said as he reached into his jacket pocket and pulled out his tape recorder. "That's why I recorded everything you said." He pressed the stop button and rewound the recorder, playing back Hatchett's confession word for word.

"You can't do this to me. I'll look like a fool! I'll have to close the park. I'll be ruined!"

"Mr. Hatchett, you can't actually expect us to feel sympathy for you," Granny said. "You are a con artist who's been lying for six hundred years. If I were you, I'd take this opportunity to change my ways, because we know the real Big Bad Wolf, and he's not as nice as our friend Puck."

"You're messing with the wrong people. The Scarlet Hand will never let you save Canis," Hatchett said as he scrambled to his feet and rushed out of the shack.

"Congratulations!" Robin said, waving his recorder in the air. "We now have proof that Canis didn't mean to kill the old woman."

"But will it matter?" Sabrina asked.

8

UNCLE JAKE DASHED OFF FOR A LATE DINNER with Briar Rose. Granny suggested everyone else get some sleep. She was sure tomorrow would be a big day in Mr. Canis's trial, perhaps even the day their friend would be released from jail. The children said good night to Granny and Elvis and climbed the steps to their bedrooms. Unfortunately, Sabrina was still handcuffed to Puck.

"Oh, I forgot about you," Puck said, eyeing the handcuffs.

"What are we going to do now, fairy boy?" Sabrina complained. "We're not sleeping in the same bed."

"You're worrying about the wrong thing, ugly. I'm going to have to go to the bathroom eventually," Puck said with a mischievous grin.

"He could sleep on the floor in our room," Daphne offered.

"I'm not sleeping on the floor. I'm royalty," Puck declared as he puffed up his chest. "Sabrina can sleep there."

"That's not going to happen," Sabrina said.

"Well, I'm definitely not sleeping there. The handcuffs have nothing to do with me," Daphne said.

Puck frowned. "Fine. Come with me."

He led the girls to his bedroom door, which was covered in signs: DEATH AWAITS ALL WHO ENTER! and WARNING! FALLING ROCKS! ANGRY DOGS! ATTACK HAMSTERS! There was also a picture of a kitten, with the words CUTENESS WILL NOT BE SPARED!

Puck's room never ceased to amaze Sabrina. Built out of magic, the bedroom was unlike any she had ever seen. The ceiling was the night sky, the ground was the forest floor, and a trickling brook led to a lagoon somewhere in the distance. Chirping crickets and the soft rustle of woodland animals drifted through the air like a lullaby. The room seemed to stretch on forever in every direction.

Puck dragged the girls down the path to a clearing littered with broken toy soldiers and parts from old skateboards and microwaves. Sabrina nearly stepped into dozens of half-eaten birthday cakes.

They climbed an embankment and found a trampoline. A panda bear was sound asleep on its bouncy surface. Puck shooed it away, and it staggered off, growling with each step.

Puck lifted Daphne onto the trampoline, then Sabrina. Together the girls pulled him up behind them.

"Wow! I love it," Daphne said, bouncing up and down happily.

"Good to know," Puck grumbled. "My only desire is ensuring the two of you are comfortable. Now, go to sleep and leave me alone."

Puck lay down, and Sabrina did the same. She nudged as far away from him as possible while still tethered to his wrist. She was supremely uncomfortable. Each time she dozed off, she felt Puck's hand drag her this way and that. Eventually, she realized that sleeping was out of the question.

"You awake?" Puck asked.

"Yes," Sabrina snapped. Her voice seemed too loud in the quiet air.

"Maybe you should tell her the truth."

Sabrina bristled. "Maybe you should mind your own business," she whispered.

Puck laughed. "As if I could! Every time I turn around, the two of you are being chased by a monster, or a robot, or a witch. Keeping you alive is a full-time job. That's why I hired the help."

His sarcasm made her even angrier. "Then why don't you go back to being a villain? I liked you a lot better when you weren't trying to save me."

"I'll go back to being a villain if you go back to the way you were," Puck said.

"And what way was that, Mr. Smarty Pants?"

"Honest," Puck said.

The word felt like a smack in the face, and Sabrina's cheeks grew hot. "You're one to talk," she mumbled.

Puck chuckled. "I am a lot of things, Sabrina—mischievous, mean-spirited, gassy—but they don't make me a bad person. They just make me immature. You stole from someone who trusted you, and then you lied about it. What do you call that?"

Sabrina wanted to get up and storm away, but the handcuffs wouldn't let her.

"What was I supposed to do, Puck? Daphne wasn't going to go get the weapon because she refuses to see what's happening to Canis. None of you want to admit the truth."

"It's obvious to most of us that furface is in trouble. I won't even say you're wrong for wanting to do something about it."

"Then what's with the lecture?"

"The way you are going about this stinks. It's noble of you to want to do the right thing, even if I think it's a waste of time. But even I know you can't make something good by doing something bad. You're Sabrina Grimm, and your sister worships you. You're supposed to be a good role model to her. Don't you think it's kind of odd that the Prince of Juvenile Delinquents is teaching you right from wrong?"

Sabrina looked off into the dark forest, not wanting to see Puck's face. She mulled over his words as she lay in the dark. She knew she had betrayed her sister, but Daphne was too young for the responsibility Hamstead had given her. Daphne always complained that Sabrina never took her opinions into consideration, which was probably why the little girl had stubbornly refused to get the weapon in the first place. But Sabrina had learned that sometimes decisions had to be made fast. If she let Daphne vote on everything, the two of them would be in a heap of trouble.

"I don't expect you to understand," Sabrina said. "It's not like you ever take my side anyway."

"Waah-waah-waah," he said. "Did I hurt your little feelings?"

"I'm used to you hurting my feelings," she grumbled.

He was silent for a long time before he spoke again. "You don't need the makeup."

Sabrina felt like her face was on fire. He knew about her late-night beauty sessions.

"So now you're going to make fun of me for that!" she snapped defensively.

"I'm not making fun of you. I'm just saying you don't need all that stuff." Puck paused. "You're pretty."

She looked over at him and found he was looking at her. They stared at each other in the dark for a very long time until they finally turned away.

"I didn't say that," Puck said, clearing his throat.

"I didn't hear a thing," Sabrina replied.

"You're a muck-covered toadface," he whispered.

"I've smelled farts sweeter than your breath," she countered.

Sabrina edged as far away as she could on the trampoline. Puck did the same.

"Hello!" Uncle Jake's voice echoed across the room.

"We're here!" Sabrina and Puck shouted in unison. The outburst woke Daphne.

"What's the big idea," she grumbled.

"Come on, kids! I found Goldilocks. She's in Paris."

The children followed their uncle into Mirror's room. In the reflection, Sabrina saw images of Paris. She marveled at its majestic architecture. The city was so gorgeous, she hadn't noticed Briar Rose sitting on the bed next to her sleeping parents. She barely had time to say hello before an excited Uncle Jake flew into a detailed explanation of Goldilocks's whereabouts.

"As you remember, Goldilocks hopped on a flight out of Venice right after the man on the motorcycle attacked her," Uncle Jake said. "Our friend Mirror discovered her destination, and we even have an exact location this time. She's checked into the Hôtel Thérèse."

"Then we don't have to go back to the library with that bumbling idiot?" Puck asked. He broke into a scratching fit, remembering his allergy to books.

"Nope. This time we can go straight to her," Uncle Jake said.

"Well, what are we waiting for?" Sabrina asked, stepping toward the traveler's chest.

"Uh, when I said we, I didn't actually mean *we*," Uncle Jake said. "You can't go."

"What? Why?" Sabrina asked.

"You're handcuffed to an Everafter, and Everafters can't leave Ferryport Landing. The traveler's chest might allow him to escape, but if not, the magic could injure him. You're going to have to stay here with Puck and Briar," Uncle Jake explained.

Sabrina now had another reason to strangle the fairy boy.

"But I can go, right?" Daphne asked.

Uncle Jake nodded. "Yes, but you'll have to stay close to me. It could be dangerous." He handed the chest's key and a slip of paper with the hotel's address to Daphne. "You want to give it a whirl this time?"

Daphne eyed the key as if it were a precious jewel. She recited the address and unlocked the chest.

"I'm so jealous!" Briar said. "I haven't been to Paris in hundreds of years."

"We'll bring you back a souvenir," Daphne promised.

Uncle Jake took his girlfriend by the hand. "If I could take you with me—"

Briar kissed him on the cheek. "Don't talk to any French girls," she warned with a smirk.

Uncle Jake winked at Briar, then turned to Daphne. "Let's scoot!"

Sabrina was livid but forced a smile. "Be careful," she told her sister.

"I'll be fine," the little girl said impatiently, rolling her eyes.

A moment later, she and Uncle Jake were gone.

"I can't believe I'm stuck here," Sabrina grumbled.

"He said we could watch them from the magic mirror," Briar said.

Mirror's face appeared in the reflection. "Hello, friends. What can I show you this evening?"

"We want to watch Uncle Jake and Daphne in Paris," Sabrina said.

"Coming right up," Mirror replied. "Just say the magic words."

"Mirror, Mirror, for goodness' sake, let me watch Uncle Jake!"

"Nice rhyme!" Mirror's face dissolved, and the reflection revealed a narrow avenue lined with elegant buildings. Each had a smoky bar, a cozy restaurant, or a fancy boutique on its ground level. People spilled out of all of them, drinking wine and gazing to the heavens, where fireworks lit up the sky. Streams of blues, greens, and reds crackled and popped around an enormous steel tower at the center of the city. At the top of the structure was a brilliant spotlight that shined three hundred and sixty degrees.

Sabrina turned to Briar to gauge her reaction. The woman was just as awestruck as she.

"So that's the Eiffel Tower," she said. "It's amazing."

Sabrina was struck by the reality of Briar's imprisonment in the little town. She couldn't visit anywhere else in the world. Paris was a place Briar never expected to see again.

Uncle Jake and Daphne appeared, stepping out of the portal and onto the avenue. They stood still for a moment, gaping at their surroundings.

"Wait! Is that her?" Briar asked, pointing to a woman walking along the cobblestone street. Sabrina looked closely. It was indeed Goldilocks, their potential savior. She was grinning from ear to ear, obviously enjoying the sights and sounds of the City of Lights.

"She's there, Jake!" Briar cried.

"Sorry, he can't hear you from here," Sabrina said. "The mirror doesn't work that way."

"How frustrating," Briar complained.

Luckily, Uncle Jake spotted Goldilocks, as well, and he and Daphne carefully followed the woman down the street.

"Not to be a downer, but what happens if she says no?" Puck chimed in. "Jake should have taken a sack in case he needs to drag her back here against her will."

Puck's words were unnerving. Sabrina hadn't thought about Goldilocks refusing to help, but now the possibility seemed all too likely. Why would the woman want to come back? Her first love was married with children. Ferryport Landing was controlled by the Scarlet Hand. She would be trapped in the town again. If

the roles were reversed, would Sabrina return? The answer was no. An army couldn't drag her back to this horrible little place.

Just then, Sabrina watched a black motorcycle tear down the street. People on the sidewalks leaped out of its way. Packages flew into the air. It was the same man from Venice! He had found Goldilocks, again. The hair on Sabrina's neck stood on end.

"Who's that maniac on the bike?" Briar asked.

"He's following Goldilocks everywhere," Sabrina explained. "He's in the Scarlet Hand."

Sabrina watched her sister and uncle bolt down the street, pushing past pedestrians and, once, knocking a waiter to the ground. Sabrina shouted for them to be careful, forgetting that no one could hear her on the other side. She should have been there helping her family, keeping Daphne safe. Sabrina had trouble breathing as she realized that this was the first time she and her sister were separated. Daphne could be injured. The lunatic on the motorcycle might hurt her. Anything could happen.

Briar seemed to sense her fear. She reached out and squeezed Sabrina's hand. "They'll be fine, Sabrina."

They watched Goldilocks spot the motorcyclist and quickly hail a taxicab. Daphne and Uncle Jake jumped into their own taxi and raced after her. With the magic mirror's image focused on her family, Sabrina couldn't see Goldilocks, but she saw the motorcycle dart past their cab. She watched Daphne crane her neck out the window to see where he was headed. When the cab made a sudden turn, the little girl nearly fell out, and Sabrina screamed.

"That was a close one," Puck laughed, but he stopped when both Sabrina and Briar flashed him an angry look. "What? It was funny."

Suddenly, like water flowing from a broken dam, stray dogs poured out of every alley and doorway. There were Rottweilers, German shepherds, Doberman pinschers, pit bulls, wolfhounds, beagles, poodles, golden retrievers, shih tzu, and dozens more in hot pursuit. They barked and snapped at the motorcyclist's feet, causing him to swerve all over the road.

"Goldilocks called some friends," Sabrina said.

"She can talk to animals?" Puck asked. "That rules."

The dogs gave the rider as much trouble as they could, but his bike was faster than all of them. Soon, they were left behind, causing traffic jams throughout much of Paris. Luckily, Uncle Jake and Daphne's cab was undeterred and their driver raced on, following Goldie's cab into a circular street called Place Charles de Gaulle. Without any traffic lights or signs, the roundabout was pure chaos, and there were several times Sabrina was sure her family would die in a head-on collision. But Goldilocks's driver was quick, and he steered the car out of traffic at the last possible second, darting down a tree-lined road.

"Where do you think she's going?" Sabrina wondered aloud.

"Exactly where I'd go," Puck said, pointing at the metal tower rising on the Parisian horizon—the Eiffel Tower.

"Why would she go up there?" Briar asked. "There's no way off once she gets to the top."

"She's probably going to pull the talking animal stunt again," Sabrina guessed. "When we tracked her down in Venice, she used a bunch of pigeons to fly her to safety. It would be a great way to lose motorcycle boy."

"Except I doubt it will work. The wind has to be crazy powerful up there. It'll be too windy to fly," Puck said.

Sabrina gasped. "So she'll be trapped?"

"Your uncle and sister will rescue her," Briar promised, though Sabrina heard uncertainty in her voice.

They watched the motorcyclist skid to a stop nearby. He leaped off his bike and pulled a silver dagger from his boot, then he raced through the tower's entrance. Uncle Jake and Daphne were close behind, but the elevator shut its doors seconds before they reached it. Climbing the stairs was out of the question; it would be too slow. They had to wait for the next lift.

When it arrived, they dashed inside, and soon they were rising up along the tower's spine. They reached the first of the tower's three platforms and raced to the second elevator. Moments later they were rising even higher above Paris.

The second level was windy, and a few people lost their hats in the strong breeze. Puck was right. Nature's forces were brutal at that height, and it wasn't even the very top of the tower.

"Look!" Puck cried as the motorcyclist came into focus. He was entering the third and final elevator. Sabrina could almost hear the chaos that ensued when he wielded his dagger and demanded everyone get off. People nearly trampled one another to get away from him. He pushed a button, and the doors closed, just as Daphne and Uncle Jake approached. The two Grimms could only stare as the elevator rose to the top of the tower. Soon the villain would have Goldilocks right where he wanted her.

"This is terrible," Briar cried.

"There will be another one soon," Sabrina said. "Don't worry."

But she was wrong. Suddenly, the elevator came crashing down from above. People screamed as smoke filled the air.

"Daphne! Uncle Jake!" Sabrina panicked but quickly spotted her sister and uncle. They were unharmed and studying the wreckage. It was obvious that the man in black had cut the cables, preventing the duo from taking that route to the top.

"He's diabolical," Briar gasped.

"And not in the good way," Puck added.

"He has Goldilocks cornered up there. They'll never get to her in time. He's going to kill her!" Sabrina cried.

"If only I were there," Briar said, pulling a small brown seed from her pocket, "one of these would be a huge help."

"I'm glad you are excited about gardening, Briar, but—"

"No, let me explain. When I was a girl, a witch put a curse on me so that if I ever pricked my finger on a spinning wheel, I would die. Well, luckily, I had a couple of fairy godmothers who fixed the magic so I would only fall asleep. To keep me safe from wild animals and nutcases, they enchanted a rosebush that grew and grew until it covered the castle. That way, nothing could get in that could harm me while I was sleeping. When William managed to cut his way through and kiss me, it broke the spell. Once I was awake, I collected some of the rosebush's seeds. They grow like crazy, and they seem to understand how I want them to grow, too. They come in handy from time to time. All you need is a handful of dirt."

"I have a handful of dirt," Puck said, reaching into his filthy pants pocket. When he pulled out his fist, he held a handful of crumbly soil. A fat earthworm was squiggling in the dirt.

"You carry dirt around with you?" Sabrina asked.

"Doesn't everyone?" Puck replied matter-of-factly.

"But what good can it do? We're in Ferryport Landing. The danger is half a world away! Unless I can get out of these handcuffs, Goldilocks is going to die," she snapped at Puck.

"Listen, I—I'm sorry I swallowed the key," he stammered. "But we have to let nature take its course."

Disgusted, Sabrina turned to the mirror. "Mirror, do we have any lock-picking stuff in the Hall of Wonders?"

Mirror's face appeared. "Sabrina, I'm increasingly concerned about your life of crime."

"It's an emergency!"

Sabrina handed him her set of keys, and moments later he returned with a small leather case. Inside were the kinds of tools Sabrina had only dreamed about when she and her sister were in foster care. There were picks of all shapes and sizes. She tried every one, jiggling each frantically into the handcuff lock while watching her uncle and sister through the mirror. Finally, when she was about to give up, the cuff clicked open. Suddenly free, she rubbed her sore wrist.

"Gimme the seed," she demanded.

"Maybe we should wake your grandmother?" Briar suggested as she hesitantly handed over her magic seed.

"No time," Sabrina said, and turned to Puck. "I need the dirt."

Puck did as he was told, and Sabrina approached the traveler's chest.

If she walked down the steps now, she'd wind up outside of the Hôtel Thérèse, far from where she needed to be, so she removed the key. "I want to go to the second-floor observation deck of the Eiffel Tower in Paris, France," she said aloud. Then she inserted the key and opened the lid. Inside, she found a completely different set of stairs.

"Be careful," Briar said. "And tell your uncle to do the same."

"I will," Sabrina called as she hurried down the stairs. At the bottom she found the door, but this one did not have a doorknob. Instead, it had a button. She pushed it and it lit up, then the door slid aside. She immediately saw her sister and uncle, and when she stepped out to greet them, she realized she was stepping out of an elevator.

"What are you doing here?" Uncle Jake asked.

"Puck finally got the key. Gross." Daphne squirmed.

"Your girlfriend sent me with some help," Sabrina said as she hurried her family to the broken elevator shaft. There, she placed Puck's dirt in a heap on the floor. She then took Briar's seed and buried it in the small pile of earth. Before she was finished, a tiny green sprout sprang out of the soil. It grew and grew, becoming plumper until it was as thick as a tree trunk and covered in roses. In a matter of seconds, it was as tall as Uncle Jake with pointy thorns sprouting out of its sides.

"My girlfriend is the coolest!" Uncle Jake said as the bush rocketed into the air. He scooped Daphne up in his arms and reached out to grab a branch. It lifted them off the ground, and together they sailed skyward as the rosebush grew at an impossible rate. "See you at the top, 'Brina."

Sabrina grabbed a vine, too. The strength of the growing bush was incredible. It nearly yanked her arm from the socket, but she held on tight. She sailed higher and higher and faster and faster until she was finally at the top of the Eiffel Tower. There, the rosebush stopped growing, and the branch eased her gently to the platform.

Sabrina stood still for a moment, trying to regain her bearings. She didn't like heights, and this tower was so high, she could feel it swaying in the powerful wind.

"She's here!" Daphne cried as she raced across the platform. Goldilocks lay on her back, motionless. Sabrina dashed to her side, with Uncle Jake in tow.

"Is she—?"

"She's alive," Uncle Jake said as he knelt to find a pulse. "She's just unconscious."

"But how?" Sabrina asked.

Before anyone could respond, the menacing motorcyclist appeared and charged across the platform at Uncle Jake. Caught off guard, Jake took several brutal punches to the face and stomach. Sabrina watched him try to fight back, but the dark rider was fast and fierce.

Sabrina and Daphne rushed to help him, but they were no match for the mysterious villain. He slapped Sabrina with a vicious backhand that sent her tumbling to the floor. When Sabrina righted herself, she realized Daphne had been hurt, too.

"Uncle Jake!" Sabrina shouted as she watched the two men circle each other.

"You must think you're pretty tough, hitting women and children," Uncle Jake said. The villain replied by lunging at him, slashing his dagger wildly. Luckily, Sabrina's uncle was fast and leaped away from each deadly attack. "And that's a snazzy outfit, hiding your face. Then again, if I were slapping around people who couldn't fight back, I'd want to hide my identity, too."

"You dare question my honor?" a muffled voice said from behind the helmet. "I'm the Black Knight, you fool."

"I thought knights rode horses," Uncle Jake challenged.

"I upgraded," the Black Knight said.

"Who knighted you?" Uncle Jake asked as he dug frantically in his pockets. "That king must have been pretty hard up for heroes."

"I serve no king," the knight growled. "Only the Master and his glorious vision of the future. When Everafters take their place as rulers of the world, your kind will be in cages, serving us."

"Blah, blah, blah," Uncle Jake mocked. "You Scarlet Hand losers sure do love the whole 'we're going to rule the world' bit. It seems to me the only thing you've got any power over is my boredom."

"Hold your tongue, fool, or I will cut it out."

At that moment, Sabrina's uncle took a small ring from his pocket and slipped it on. "Well, pal, if you're feeling froggy, take a leap."

The Black Knight dove for Uncle Jake, and the two men tumbled over each other. Sabrina watched Jake lock his hand around the knight's wrist and knock the dagger from his grip. But the knight's other hand was free, and he punched Uncle Jake several times in the jaw. Every time the knight seemed to get the upper hand, Uncle Jake managed to pummel him and gain control, but it never lasted long. The Black Knight was obviously stronger than Uncle Jake and a much better fighter. Sabrina could only watch in horror when the dark villain clenched his free hand around Jake's throat to choke him. Daphne tried to scramble over and lend a hand, but Sabrina held her back.

"Leave him alone!" Sabrina begged, but the knight ignored her. He continued to squeeze, and Jake's face turned blue. In desperation, Jake raised his hand to the knight's face, and a blast of red-hot magic blasted from the tiny ring on his pinky finger. It temporarily blinded Sabrina but didn't seem to faze the Black Knight in the least.

"My Master prepared me for your silly tricks, fool," he said.

Uncle Jake gasped and his eyes bulged. The knight was killing him, and there was no one to stop him—no one except for Sabrina. She reached in her pocket for the kazoo and took a deep breath, hoping she could direct its power at the knight without harming her uncle. She couldn't be sure, but she didn't have a choice. She blew as hard as her lungs would allow, and howling wind swirled around the villain. It lifted the Black Knight off the floor, and in his confusion, he released Uncle Jake. The wind carried the knight over the edge of the platform, and he dropped out of sight into nothingness. Sabrina heard his fading screams and rushed to the railing. She had never planned to kill him, and the horror of what had just happened tightened her chest. Luckily, the knight was alive, trapped in the vines of the enchanted rosebush.

Sabrina rushed to Uncle Jake's side and helped him sit up. The man's face was red and he coughed violently, but she was sure he would be OK. Daphne attended to Goldilocks, calling out her name until she woke.

"What happened?" the woman asked.

"Don't worry," Daphne assured her. "You're safe now. The Black Knight is gone."

"It's you!" Goldilocks said when she spotted Jake. She looked startled at first but then smiled.

"You want me to come back," she said apprehensively. Uncle Jake tried to speak but couldn't. All he could do was nod his head.

"We need your help, and we wouldn't ask if there was any other way," Sabrina said.

"Who are you?" Goldilocks stood and looked from one sister to the next.

"I'm Sabrina, and this is my sister, Daphne. We're Henry Grimm's daughters."

Goldilocks studied their faces closely. "I see a lot of him in you," she told Daphne, then looked at Sabrina. "So he married her, huh? You're the spitting image."

Sabrina nodded. "Her name is Veronica. She's our mother."

Goldilocks gave a sad little smile and got to her feet. She gave Uncle Jake a hug. "It's good to see you, Jakey."

Uncle Jake nodded and smiled, then pointed at his throat.

"The knight tried to strangle him," Daphne explained.

"Tell me Henry's safe," Goldilocks pleaded. Sabrina could see the woman still cared strongly for her father. She wasn't sure how to react.

"He's not dead, if that's what you're asking, but he does need you," Daphne said. "He's trapped under a sleeping spell, and we need you to kiss him. That is, if you still love him."

Goldilocks blushed. "This sounds like a job for your mother."

Sabrina shook her head. "She's asleep, too."

"Never a dull moment in Ferryport Landing," the blond beauty said. "How did this happen?"

"The Scarlet Hand did it," Uncle Jake croaked.

"The Scarlet who?" the blonde asked.

"They're bad guys," Daphne said. "They kidnapped Mom and Dad almost two years ago. Now they're running the town. That creepy guy, the Black Knight, he's one of them."

"He's been chasing me for a month," Goldilocks explained.

"If you come back, we'll protect you," Sabrina said.

"Come back to Ferryport Landing?"

Sabrina nodded hopefully.

Goldilocks turned toward the horizon. "I can't do that. Terrible things happened to set me free. Your grandfather died because of it. Going back would mean it was all for nothing. I'm sure your father would rather stay asleep than accept my help. He told me he never wanted to see me again."

"But without you it's impossible," Daphne said.

"I'm sorry. I wish I could help. Don't give up hope. You live in Ferryport Landing. Anything is possible there." She turned and walked down the steps. Sabrina started after her, but Uncle Jake grabbed her arm, pulling her back. He shook his head. "Let her go," he croaked.

"We have to make her understand."

"She's made her choice," he said.

"Then we'll force her to go back with us," Sabrina cried.

"That's not what we do," he said gently.

"But—"

Daphne shook her head. "Hand it over," she demanded.

Sabrina shuffled her feet. "What, the kazoo?"

"It's magic, Sabrina. You can't handle it. Give it to me."

"But—"

Daphne shook her head. "Don't argue with me. Just hand it over."

Sabrina dug into her pocket for the kazoo. Her fingers tingled when she touched it. It made her feel good, but she knew that feeling was dangerous. Her sister was right. Daphne took it without a word, and she walked down the steps, helping her uncle along the way.

9

UNCLE JAKE PACKED UP THE TRAVELER'S CHEST, and the same tortoise and hare who'd delivered it came to pick it up. The hare hoisted it onto his partner's shell and walked it over to their truck. Moments later, they were gone, along with the only hope the family had of ever seeing Goldilocks again.

"None of you care whether Mom and Dad ever wake up!" Sabrina shrieked at her family. She raced upstairs to the room where her parents slept, nestled herself between their bodies, and sobbed. Her familiar thoughts of hatred toward Everafters surfaced. Most were traitors; others couldn't be counted on. She wept openly, not caring if Mirror or anyone else heard. Mirror's face appeared briefly in the reflection but then faded away just as quickly. She silently thanked him for letting her be alone. She lay there for hours, until all her tears were spent.

She got to her feet and went out into the hallway, where she found Granny, Uncle Jake, Briar, and Elvis sitting on the hardwood floor, obviously waiting for her.

Granny took her by the hand. "Sabrina—"

Sabrina pulled away. "I can't take a lecture right now."

"No lecture. I was going to say I'm sorry. I know how heartbroken you must feel. We feel it, too, dear. We all had the same hopes you did."

Sabrina nodded sadly. "Where's Daphne?"

"She's in your room," the old woman said.

"You might want to give her some time," Uncle Jake said.

"Why?"

"She's a little angry right now," he replied.

"I know how she feels," Sabrina said, ignoring the warning. She walked to their bedroom. There, she found Daphne sitting at Henry's desk, braiding her own hair into familiar pigtails. She was no longer wearing Sabrina's clothes and had gone back to her old pair of cotton candy–colored pajamas with little stars on them. Her face was scrubbed clean of the lip gloss.

"I can't believe we're not going to drag Goldilocks back here," Sabrina said.

"I'd rather not talk to you, Sabrina," the little girl said.

Sabrina was taken aback by her sister's attitude. "You're angry about the weapon. I can explain—"

"I said I don't want to talk about it," Daphne interrupted.

"Well, I think we should. I want to explain."

Daphne burst into tears. "How are you going to explain that you stole from me and lied about it? How are you going to explain that you . . . that you betrayed me?"

"You don't even know what *betrayed* means!"

"Yes, I do!" Daphne said, heaving a new pocket dictionary at her sister. "I looked it up."

Sabrina bent down and picked up her sister's dictionary. "Yes, I lied to you. I stole the key and snuck out and took the weapon. You're too young to have that kind of responsibility, and you refused to see the danger we are in, so I had to."

"You treat me like I'm a baby, Sabrina. I'm not a baby!"

"You are a baby! Mocking me by walking around here in my clothes and playing dress-up doesn't make you an adult."

"I wasn't mocking you, Sabrina. I was trying to be more like you. You were my role model, dummy," Daphne snapped. "But not anymore. I think I'll go back to being myself. I like me."

Sabrina looked at the stack of her clothing on the bed.

"You don't like me?" she asked.

"Not right now," the little girl said. "And it's pretty obvious that you don't like me, either."

"That's not true!" Sabrina said.

"You can't like someone you don't respect, Sabrina," Daphne

said. "Well, don't worry. You don't have to look after your baby sister any longer. I'm moving into Granny's room tonight. And, tomorrow, Mr. Boarman and Mr. Swineheart are coming over to build me my own bedroom."

She finished braiding her hair and got up from the desk.

"I have something of yours," Daphne continued, placing a tube of lip gloss in Sabrina's hand as she walked past her into the hallway and closed the door behind her.

Sabrina bit her lip so hard, she tasted blood. Puck was right all along. He'd warned her that the truth would come out and that, when it did, it would be ugly. That was the only thing he got wrong—it wasn't just ugly, it was horrible.

The next morning, Robin and Little John arrived bright and early with more bad news.

"The tape is missing," Robin explained. "Everything Hatchett said is gone. We've got no evidence!"

"What happened?" Granny Relda demanded.

"We don't know, but we have our suspicions," Robin said. "You know that caterpillar on the jury, the one always smoking a hookah with the Scarlet Hand mark on his chest?"

"Sure," Daphne said.

"Well, this morning when I woke up, the tape was gone, and the whole place reeks of apple tobacco."

"There aren't a lot of pipe-smoking caterpillars in this town," Uncle Jake said.

"We've got no chance of saving Canis if the jury is trying to sabotage our case," Little John replied.

"Sadly, that's not even our biggest worry. Bluebeard is calling Red Riding Hood to testify. She's going to back up Hatchett's story," Robin said.

"Maybe not," Daphne said as she removed the kazoo from her pocket. "I have an idea that might put a whammy into Bluebeard's case."

"A whammy?" Robin Hood asked.

"It's my new word. It means something no one sees coming."

Little John scooped Daphne up into his arms. "Well, young lady, we could really use a whammy right about now!"

Nurse Sprat seemed startled when the group returned to the hospital.

"You want to see her again? No one ever wants to see her again."

"We're gluttons for punishment," Sabrina said as the nurse led them to Red's room.

"I'm worried about this plan," Robin said. "Daphne has never used this magic kazoo before, and if what Sabrina says is true, it can demolish a house with one little puff."

"It kind of does what you want it to," Sabrina explained. "If you concentrate."

"Except for the time you destroyed the bank," Puck reminded her.

"Fine! Fifty percent of the time it works like a charm."

"I'm still a bit confused," Little John said. "Are you planning to blow this crazy child to smithereens? What good will that do us?"

"It does more than blow houses down," Daphne said. "It cures the mentally ill."

"Uh, maybe you should turn it on yourself, 'cause you sound crazy," Puck commented.

"We know that Red's mother sent her into the forest with a basket of food to deliver to her grandma. That part of the story has always seemed a little odd. Who sends a child into the woods by herself? That is not good parenting."

"Good point," Uncle Jake said.

"I think Red's family was at their wit's end because she was sick. They sent her to her grandmother's house because she had magic to make Red better. I don't think this kazoo is a weapon. I think it was meant to be medicine. I believe it can actually blow the mental illness out of a person," Daphne explained. "Nurse Sprat, would you happen to have an empty jar with a tight lid?"

"Why?" Sprat asked.

"Let's just say it's going to make your job here at the hospital a lot easier."

Sprat shrugged. "I'll check," she said, as she opened the door that led to Red's room.

"You came back," Red said excitedly, when she saw the family. "Please, sit, have some tea!"

"I'd love some." Daphne sat down at the table with the kazoo in hand. Sabrina stood behind her, fists clenched in case the little maniac flew into a rage and tried to attack Daphne.

"Red, do you remember when we said you were sick inside your brain?" Daphne asked.

Red nodded.

"Well, how would you like to feel better?"

Red clapped. "Then I can go home to my mommy and daddy."

"They wanted you to get better," Daphne said to the deranged girl. Red smiled and hugged a doll with a missing head.

"Daphne, are you sure about this?" Granny asked.

"Almost positive," Daphne said. "We all remember what Hatchett said about the day Red's grandmother died. He and Canis stumbled upon the old lady's house. They watched her blow a dark shadow out of the rabid wolf, and then it was suddenly tame. She wasn't just being kind to an animal. She was testing her magic. When it worked, she bottled the bad stuff up and got ready to do the same thing to her granddaughter."

"She was trying to fix Red," Granny marveled. "Daphne, this is a very clever bit of detective work."

Uncle Jake nodded. "So, Mr. Canis, or Tobias Clay—or whatever his real name is—he just got in the way. He was trying to be a hero and save Red, but the wolf's madness got loose and infected him. That's how he became the Big Bad Wolf. He's the real hero woodcutter from the story, not Howard Hatchett!"

"What happens if Red's madness slips into one of us just like the wolf's went into Canis?" Little John asked. "Canis has never been able to fully control it."

"We have to be careful," Daphne said.

There was a knock at the door, and when it opened, Nurse Sprat was there, nervously holding a glass jar.

"Here! Will this work? Good!" she cried, shoving it into Sabrina's hands before slamming the door tight.

"I hope so," Sabrina said, finally understanding Daphne's plan.

"If the Three Pigs had trapped the Wolf's madness in something, we might have been rid of the monster for good," Daphne explained. "But they didn't know what the kazoo could really do. They thought it was just the secret behind his huffing and puffing. When they unleashed it on him, they blew the madness away for a moment, leaving our Canis behind."

"But why didn't Mr. Canis lose total control again?"

Daphne shrugged. "Maybe knocking the Wolf loose was all Canis needed to regain control over his own body."

"And it was only when he fought Jack and tasted his blood that the Wolf got the upper hand again," Granny said. "This is all starting to make sense."

"So, you think that if you blow Red's madness out of her, she'll be able to remember the day her grandmother died more clearly?" Sabrina asked.

"No. I mean, maybe," Daphne said. "Mr. Canis has no memories of who he was before the pigs gave him the beatdown. Red might not remember anything at all."

"The upside is she won't be able testify against Canis," Little John said.

"I'm not sure I like this idea," Puck said. "What if you erase her mind completely? Some memories are sacred. I'd be heartbroken if I forgot every fart I've ever let loose."

"He's got a point, Daphne," Granny said. "She might be a blank slate when this is over."

"It's worth the risk. We need someone to stand up for Mr. Canis in court, and who better than the person he's accused of hurting the most?" Daphne said.

"Are we talking about the doggy?" Red asked.

"Yes. Do you want to help the doggy, Red?" Granny Relda asked the little girl, gently. "Do you want to get better so that you can leave the hospital? I think we can help."

"Yes," said Red with a nod. "I want to go home."

"Do it," Sabrina said to her sister. "When I turned the kazoo on the Black Knight, I concentrated on having the power affect only him. I think the wind will do what you ask, but you have to focus."

Daphne raised the kazoo to her lips and blew. The wind blasted out of it, upending the dolls, tea set, and anything that wasn't nailed down. Red, however, seemed unfazed, except for her hair flying around. She glanced around her and laughed.

"Bad weather!" she shrieked. "Very bad weather."

The wind swept around her like a snake. It crept around every limb, embraced her tightly, and then reached down her throat. She screamed as something horrible and black climbed out of her mouth. To call it a person would be wrong. It was more like an animal, with eyes like bottomless pits. To Sabrina, it looked like some horribly mutated worm seeking revenge on a fisherman. It whipped around violently in midair, fighting against the force determined to separate it from Red Riding Hood.

"Now, Sabrina!" Daphne cried.

Sabrina opened the glass jar to trap the creature. It thrashed about as she forced it into the jar. She quickly tightened the lid, and the wind vanished. She watched her sister slip the kazoo back into her pocket. Red Riding Hood collapsed to the floor and lay still.

"She's hurt," Robin Hood said, rushing to her side, but his

concerns proved unwarranted. Red slowly opened her eyes and looked up into Granny Relda's face.

"Grandmother?" she asked.

Sabrina's heart sank. Red was just as crazy as before. The weapon had not done what they had hoped.

The door to the room flew open and slammed against the wall. Bluebeard and Nottingham barged in, along with half a dozen card guards armed with swords.

"Sorry, Grimms!" Nottingham said. "We have to take our witness to the trial."

One of the card guards dragged Red from the room.

"I do hope you had enough time to question her," Bluebeard said. "Though I suspect you didn't get too many straight answers."

"The trial starts in fifteen minutes," Nottingham called back over his shoulder. "See you in court."

The family pushed their way through the crowd at the entrance to the courtroom. There were no seats and barely any standing room left.

Mayor Heart made her way over to the Grimms. She wore a wicked grin that made Sabrina's stomach turn. "Looks like today's the day we wrap this all up, Grimms. I suspect your Wolf will meet the hangman by this time tomorrow."

"Isn't she a delight?" Granny commented sarcastically when the mayor walked away.

Judge Hatter entered the courtroom and made his way to his desk, now just a stack of milk crates. He didn't seem to notice. The Four of Spades called for order.

"Let's get started," Judge Hatter said. "We can't exactly get ended, can we? No, I suppose we can't. Can we? Or is it, may we? We may. No, we may not. Mr. Bluebeard, do you have a new witness?"

Bluebeard stood up from his desk and surveyed the crowd. He beamed an insincere smile at everyone, including Sabrina and her family. "Indeed, I do. In fact, she's my last witness. I call Little Red Riding Hood to the stand."

The crowd fell silent. The double doors in the courtroom opened, and a card guard escorted Red to the stand. He helped her into her seat and stood nearby, watching her closely.

"Does the witness need to be watched?" Hatter asked.

The card guard nodded. "This one is especially dangerous. She's mentally ill, sir."

"Oh, how exciting!" Hatter sang with delight. "What does she do? Eat people? Push them out of windows? Throw knives?"

"All of the above, I believe."

"Bluebeard, please proceed."

The lawyer approached the little girl, but even he kept a safe distance. Red just sat there, gazing around as if lost in thought.

"Precious girl," Bluebeard started. "You have been through so much. I hate to put you through any more, but we need to get to the truth. We have a . . . ahem . . . man on trial for his life, so I hope you'll be brave and answer some questions."

Red continued gazing about. Sabrina had seen this dazed expression before. The little lunatic was probably having another delusion.

"Red, we've already established that your parents sent you to see your grandmother with a basket of food. Do you know why they sent you?"

"Momma told me Granny was sick," Red said.

"Your grandmother was sick? How sad. So, you went through the woods to her house. When you got there, what did you see?"

"A monster," Red said.

Bluebeard smiled. "Can you point out that monster?"

Without so much as a moment of hesitation, Red pointed at Mr. Canis.

"Let the record show that the child pointed at the accused," the lawyer said, then turned back to Red. "Where was your grandmother when you arrived?"

"The Wolf ate her," Red said softly.

"That's terrible," Bluebeard said. He looked as if he might burst into tears, but Sabrina knew he was acting. "I'm sure you know this, but your story has been spread far and wide. In one version, you came into the house and found the Wolf hiding in your grandmother's bed. Is that what happened?"

"Yes," Red said.

"Why would he do that?" Bluebeard asked.

"He wanted to trick me so he could eat me, too," Red said.

"Luckily, a woodcutter came and saved your life," Bluebeard said as he turned to the jury. His face was beaming with confidence.

"No, that's not what happened."

Bluebeard's face fell. He spun around to face Red once more.

"I'm sorry, child. Maybe you misunderstood what I said. I was talking about the brave woodcutter who saved your life."

Red shook her head. "I heard what you said. I said that isn't what happened. I found the woodcutter hiding in the fields."

"Then how did you escape the Wolf?" Bluebeard asked.

"I didn't have to. He saved me," Red said, pointing at Mr. Canis.

The crowd broke into excited chatter. Hatter slammed a gavel down on the stack of milk crates. They collapsed before him. With nothing to bang on, he pounded the gavel into his own head. "Order!"

"The jury should be careful about what the witness says. She's mentally ill," Bluebeard said.

"Objection!" Robin Hood cried. "If her testimony can't be trusted, then why is she here?"

"Order!" Hatter shrieked. "Mr. Bluebeard, do you have any more questions?"

Bluebeard looked frantic. "No, sir!"

Judge Hatter, however, had some of his own. "You say the creature who murdered your grandmother saved your life?"

Red nodded. "My grandmother was trying to heal my mind. She was a witch, and she had a plan, but it went wrong and she accidentally created the Big Bad Wolf. That poor man, the one they call Mr. Canis, was the real victim. He was in the wrong place at the wrong time. He didn't mean to kill my grandmother, but he couldn't stop the Wolf. Lucky for me, he got control over the Wolf for a brief moment and begged me to run."

"They say you've got a broken brain," Hatter said. "I know crazy, and you seem perfectly fine to me."

Red scanned the crowd and found Sabrina and her family. She smiled. "I'm feeling much better now."

Sabrina looked to her grandmother. The old woman was grinning from ear to ear and squeezing Daphne's hand.

"It worked!" Daphne cheered.

"Objection!" Bluebeard cried. "We are finished with this witness."

Judge Hatter snarled at Bluebeard. "I say when a witness is ready to go."

"It's true that the Wolf killed my grandmother, but I don't think he could control himself. I know how that feels. I've done terrible things, too. The Wolf is dangerous, but the man is not. Mr. Canis does not deserve to die."

"Objection!" Mayor Heart roared from her seat.

"Your Honor, we rest our case," Bluebeard said frantically.

Hatter shrugged. "Fine with me. We'll take a one-hour break and come back to hear the jury's decision."

"So we don't get to question this witness, either?" Robin Hood protested.

"Objection!" Hatter shouted.

"I beg your pardon," said the bewildered lawyer.

"I object," the judge replied.

"You're the judge. You don't get to object," Robin cried.

"Well, I object to not being allowed to object. I find it . . . objectionable," Hatter replied. "The court finds the Wolf not guilty!" He slammed his head with the gavel and prepared to leave.

"Your Honor!" Bluebeard exclaimed. "The jury has to vote on whether the Wolf is guilty. You can't do that yourself."

"I really do not like this game," the judge said. "I'm going to lunch. I'll be back in one hour."

Judge Hatter got off his chair and raced through the aisle toward the double doors. Sabrina watched him pass, marveling that his neck could support his monstrous head and nose. For a head so big, there weren't that many thoughts inside it.

The family congregated at Briar Rose's coffee shop. Briar took a break to sit with them, but not before she brought everyone fresh muffins and steaming-hot beverages. Sabrina, Puck, and

Daphne enjoyed cocoa with whipped cream and watched Briar's fairy godmothers stew with anger when the princess kissed Uncle Jake hello.

"They're going to turn me into a frog," Uncle Jake said.

"Well, I won't be the first princess in this town to fall in love with one," Briar bantered.

"What do you think our friend's chances are?" Uncle Jake asked Granny.

The old woman sipped her coffee. "Who can say? The judge is a wild card."

"The judge is a certifiable loony tune," Puck agreed.

Granny nodded. "But he doesn't seem to be in Mayor Heart's pocket. I think they thought that having an insane person as the judge might sway things in their favor, but it's not turning out that way. He's proving to be unpredictable for us all. And then there's Mr. Charming on the jury. I'm hoping he'll vote to free Canis."

"Mom, he's joined the Scarlet Hand now," Uncle Jake said. "Not that I'm surprised. Charming always went whichever way the wind was blowing. He'll do what's in his best interests. And it's not like he and Canis were friends."

Sabrina had no idea what Charming might do. His joining the Scarlet Hand had come as the biggest surprise yet, even if he had said he would do anything to protect Snow White. Sabrina just couldn't have guessed he'd go so far.

Just then, one of Robin's merry men came running into the coffee shop. He was so out of breath, he could barely speak.

"The . . . jury . . . is . . . back," he gasped. "Robin and Little John need you back at the courthouse, now!"

The double doors were closed and two card guards blocked the way when the family arrived.

"Court is in session. No one may enter," the Eight of Diamonds said.

"You let me in right now, or I swear the two of you will get the shuffling of your lives," Granny threatened.

Stunned, the guards stepped aside, and Granny threw the doors open. Every person in the packed courtroom turned to gape at the noisy newcomers.

"Um, as I was saying," Judge Hatter said. "Has the jury reached a verdict?"

Charming stood up. He held a folded piece of paper in his hands. "We have, Your Honor," he said.

"C'mon, Billy," Snow muttered to herself. "Do the right thing. I know you're a good person."

"Very good. Read your verdict," Hatter replied.

Charming cleared his throat and unfolded the paper. "We, the jury, find the accused . . . guilty of murder."

Snow gasped. "Oh, Billy."

Most of the audience cheered. The noise banged against Sabrina's eardrums like a wooden spoon on an old pot. She felt dizzy and sick to her stomach. Granny and Daphne looked no better.

"I see," Hatter said when the crowd grew quiet. "Then I suppose we need to sentence him, and I tell you folks, I'm going to give him a full sentence. Not a sentence fragment, but a complete sentence with a verb and a noun and quite possibly an adjective. I wouldn't be surprised if there was a conjunction in there, too. Thus, I sentence the Wolf to death by hanging!"

The crowd leaped to its feet. Some were dancing and clapping; others laughed and howled with twisted joy. Sabrina needed all of her strength just to stay upright.

"Order! Order in the court!" Hatter cried, striking his head with his gavel again. "The Wolf will be hanged in the center of town tomorrow at noon. This trial is adjourned!"

Hatter rushed out of the room. Bluebeard, however, stood beaming at the Grimms. Robin Hood and Little John pushed through the crowd to the family. Their long faces spoke a thousand words of remorse. Granny thanked them for trying, then hurried to speak to Mr. Canis before card guards dragged him away.

"Old friend!"

"Old friend," Canis said, his features now almost completely those of the Wolf.

"We'll work on another way," Granny said. "There's no reason to worry."

Canis shook his head. "It's over, Relda. This is how I want it."

He allowed the guards to lead him out of the courtroom.

Daphne hugged her grandmother and wept into the old woman's dress. Tears were rolling down Granny's face, as well. Uncle Jake was shaken and pale. Puck, however, was furious.

"I'm going to rescue him!" he shouted angrily. His wings sprang from his back and his eyes turned coal black. He snatched his sword from his waist and flew toward the door that Canis had exited through, but Granny pulled him back by his foot.

"No, Puck!"

"He needs our help, old lady!" Puck shouted.

"No! Not here. Not this way. If you go after him, they will arrest you next. I can't bear to lose another member of my family."

"What now?" Sabrina asked. For the first time since she had met the old woman, Granny Relda was dumbstruck. Her gaze was fixed on something at the far end of the room. Sabrina followed it to find Charming staring back at them. Bluebeard joined him and shook his hand, as did Heart and Nottingham.

Snow White saw it, as well. She bit her lower lip, and a tear rolled down her cheek. She turned to Granny Relda.

"I'm sorry," she whispered. "I can't be here."

Snow turned and ran out of the room. Charming watched her

go without a word. Sabrina glared at the man as if he were mold on the bottom of a toilet. He had tricked her. Daphne had always believed he was a hero, but Sabrina had never fully trusted him. She hated that her instincts had been right.

10

O N THE DAY THE BIG BAD WOLF WAS sentenced to die, it rained. Buckets of water poured from heavy black clouds and flooded the streets. The town's drainage system backed up, and water flowed through the tiny hamlet without restraint.

Granny Relda had wrapped herself in a rain jacket, and Uncle Jake stood beside her holding an umbrella over her head. She wanted the children to stay home but realized they'd sneak out anyway. She agreed to let them come along to say good-bye to Mr. Canis, but they were not to watch the execution. Sabrina knew it would be her last chance to apologize to the man who had protected her family for almost two decades. She wanted to tell him how wrong she'd been about him.

The family drove to Main Street in their old car. Sabrina sat, remembering how noisy the car had been with Canis behind the wheel. She would miss the screeching brakes and loud backfires.

In the center of Main Street, a large platform had been constructed. It had two levels: one was wide and close to the ground, and the second was at the top of a tower, high above the other. A noose swung from a post above the second platform.

A huge crowd was already gathered. Sabrina and her family moved to the front as Everafters shouted filthy insults at them: The Grimms were a blight and a menace. They were disgusting, repulsive humans. They were inferior and stupid and the root of everyone's suffering.

Bluebeard, Nottingham, Mayor Heart, and Charming appeared on the first platform. The crowd cheered, and Heart waved like she was in a beauty pageant.

"We've waited a long time for this, haven't we?" she shouted into her megaphone. The crowd roared with approval, and she turned her attention to Sabrina and her family. "But trust me, people. Today is just the beginning. Bring out the Wolf!"

The crowd broke into a chant of "Bring out the Wolf!"

Half a dozen card guards appeared with Canis in their midst. He towered over them, but he didn't look as if he were going to put up a fight. The guards led him up to the second platform, and the Ace of Spades wrapped the noose around his thick, hairy neck.

"I'd like to speak to my friend," Granny said. She pushed her way to the tower and climbed the stairs.

"You'll be up there yourself soon!" someone shouted.

Sabrina watched her grandmother talk to Canis. She couldn't hear what the old woman was saying, but it was obvious to her that Granny was begging him to escape. He shook his head and spoke to her softly.

"What is she doing?" a voice asked from behind them. Sabrina turned to find Snow White.

"I think she's trying to convince him to make a run for it," Uncle Jake said.

"He doesn't seem to be listening," Snow said.

"That's because he's smart," another voice said. This one belonged to Bluebeard, who was standing uncomfortably close to the beautiful teacher. "Personally, I think he welcomes the opportunity to end his suffering. He's committed so many atrocities. It must be hard on his soul."

"You would know," Snow spat.

Bluebeard's face turned crimson, but he composed himself and even laughed.

Sabrina couldn't stand to be near the villain any longer. She snatched her sister's hand, and together they climbed the tower to Granny and Canis.

"Girls, it's not safe," the old woman protested.

"I need to say good-bye," Sabrina said.

"Me, too," Daphne added.

"I have been very rude to you. I have never treated you with the respect you deserve," Sabrina said to Canis as she turned to her sister. "It's a problem I have. I seem to treat everyone badly."

"You are young, Sabrina Grimm," Canis said. "Time will supply you with wisdom. I'm sorry I will not be around to see how you use it."

Daphne clung to Canis and hugged him tightly. "Good-bye, Tobias Clay."

Canis looked confused.

"That was your name, before. You were a man once, free of the monster," Sabrina explained.

Canis shook his head. "A man? Is that true? I don't remember anything before the incident. Did I have a wife? Children? Who was I?"

"We don't know," Sabrina said.

Mr. Canis seemed shocked. "If only I had known—"

"Get your children down now!" Heart bellowed through her megaphone.

Granny said one final good-bye and ushered the girls down the steps.

"Does the prisoner have any last words?" Heart shouted.

Canis looked out at the crowd and laughed.

"What's so funny, mongrel?"

"Look at all the monsters," he said.

Heart snarled and pulled a lever. The floor beneath Canis

slid open, and his body fell like a stone. Sabrina knew the image would haunt her for the rest of her life, but she couldn't help watching. Luckily, what she saw was not so tragic. Canis landed on his feet. The rope was sliced in two, and an arrow buried itself in the ground behind the platform. The crowd gasped and turned their attention away from the gallows. Standing across the street was Robin Hood, no longer in his suit and tie, but in a tunic and tights. He was holding a bow with a second arrow trained on Mayor Heart. Little John stood next to him wielding a long wooden staff. The rest of the merry men gathered behind them.

"Hood!" Nottingham raged.

"Did you miss us?" Robin asked with a grin, then waved to the crowd. "For those of you wondering, the Sherwood Group is officially shuttered. But don't worry about us; we'll find other jobs. You know what they say, 'Do what you love and the money will come.' I look forward to robbing all of you in the very near future."

"That guy is so cool," Puck said.

Nottingham drew his dagger. "I'll kill you, Robin. This time I'll make sure of it." He pushed through the crowd, shoving people to the ground in his eagerness to reach the outlaw.

Robin and his merry men didn't wait. They rushed into the crowd, as well, turning it into an enormous riot. Everyone was fighting—members of the Scarlet Hand even fought one another.

"We have to get out of here," Uncle Jake said, reaching into his pockets to arm himself with magical items.

"What about Mr. Canis?" Daphne asked as she scanned the crowd for his familiar face.

Sabrina could see the huge man tossing people aside and roaring. "I see Canis. I think he's OK."

"Are we all here?" Granny asked.

Sabrina scanned the crowd. "Where's Ms. White?"

In the chaos, even a trained self-defense teacher like Snow could be seriously injured. Sabrina shouted at Puck. "Hey, dirtface. Find Snow White!"

Puck nodded and zipped away, using the opportunity to smack the tops of people's heads with his wooden sword. While he searched, Uncle Jake and Granny pulled Briar, her fairy godmothers, and the girls to safety. It wasn't easy. Swords and daggers slashed the air. Wands and magic lit up the sky.

"This is insane," Sabrina cried. "The whole town is at war."

Suddenly, Puck returned, and he looked worried. "I found Snow. She's in trouble. Follow me!"

The family raced after the flying boy. He led them a block away, where they found Bluebeard dragging Ms. White into a dark alley.

"Leave her alone!" Daphne shouted as they approached.

Bluebeard sneered. "You people run along. Snow and I are going to have a little talk about manners."

While he was distracted, Snow punched him in the face and he fell backward, only to spring back to his feet. He wrapped his arm around her neck and pulled a dagger from his pocket. He ran its tip along Snow's delicate throat.

"Let's not get excited. I'd hate for someone to lose their head," Bluebeard threatened. "Snow and I need to come to an understanding. She has been very cruel to me, and I demand an apology."

"I don't know what you're talking about, Bluebeard," Snow said.

"I asked you on a date like a gentleman, and you coldly rejected me. I will not be humiliated."

"You disgust me!" Snow cried.

Sabrina heard someone running toward them. She spun around to find Charming approaching from Main Street.

"Billy!" Snow cried.

"Charming," Bluebeard said. "Have they captured the Wolf yet?"

"No, not yet," Charming said. "He's putting up a good fight."

"I was just having a conversation with Snow about how to respect other people," Bluebeard said.

"I see. How is it going?"

"Not well. I wanted to give your ex a chance to redeem herself. She's no friend of the Hand, what with her relationship with these

lousy Grimms. I had hoped that if she were involved with me, it might save her life when the Master rises, but she will not see reason."

"It's hopeless. I've tried," Charming said, approaching them.

"William, you don't mind if I have a little fun with her, do you?" Bluebeard asked. "You did say you were done with her now that you've pledged allegiance to the Master."

Charming went still, then nodded.

Sabrina couldn't believe her eyes. Serving his own interests was no surprise, but betraying the one person he'd sworn to love was something she'd never thought Charming would do. Had the Hand brainwashed him?

He turned back to the family and took a sword from his belt. While Bluebeard hurt Snow, it was clear he was going to take care of Sabrina and her family.

"William, no!" Briar screamed.

In one lightning-fast move, Charming whipped around and plunged his weapon into Bluebeard's side. The villain looked at him for a long, pained moment, then collapsed with the blade still in his torso. His eyes closed, and he was still.

"He did it," Daphne said. "He changed the future."

Snow trembled when Charming pulled her to his side. "You hate me," he said. "I get that. And I would apologize, but I can't. I did all of this—the betrayal, the cruelty, joining this wretched Hand—to save your life."

Charming turned to Granny. "Canis has fled."

"What? Where did he go?"

"Robin spoke to him about that fool Hatchett. Canis was furious. Something inside him snapped, and he ran off vowing to kill him," he said. "I think he's totally lost control of the Wolf."

Granny took Daphne's hand. "Do you still have that kazoo?"

The little girl nodded.

"C'mon. It might be our only chance to stop another tragedy."

A caravan containing the family, Charming, Snow, Briar, Robin, and his merry men raced through the twisting country roads of Ferryport Landing toward Hatchettland.

When they arrived, everyone raced into the park.

"Do you think we beat him here?" Robin asked.

Somewhere down the path, Hatchett screamed, and there was a terrible roar.

"I wouldn't bet money on it," Puck said as he grabbed his sword. He ran down the path.

"Puck, it's too dangerous!" Granny shouted after him.

"There's no way I'm missing this!" he cried. "If the Wolf eats him, I want a front-row seat."

Everyone followed the path to the ancient house. Once there, Sabrina could see the door had been ripped off its hinges and tossed aside. Puck was waiting outside with his sword in hand.

"Children, you are to keep your distance from Mr. Canis," Granny said, then turned to Daphne. "Are you ready?"

Daphne held up the kazoo and nodded.

Granny called out to Mr. Canis. There was no response, so she called out to the Wolf. A moment later, the hulking creature stomped through the doorway, dragging Hatchett behind him. The man kicked and screamed and begged to be saved.

"Can you believe this guy? He built this place to honor his bravery," the Wolf said. "The brave hero who supposedly destroyed me is sobbing like a baby."

"Let Mr. Hatchett go, please," Granny begged.

The Wolf chuckled. "Relda, you tried to help Canis keep me locked up, so you know me very well. I'm back in action, and I'm eager to spill some blood."

"I know Mr. Canis is still in there," Granny said. "He'll stop you."

"You're right, Relda. Come closer and take my hand. Maybe you can coax him out. C'mon, give it a try. See what happens."

"Let the man go!" Robin Hood shouted. His bow was loaded with an arrow and aimed at the Wolf's chest.

"We're going to give you one last chance to stop," Granny said sternly.

The Wolf raised his eyebrows in surprise. "Relda, you're threatening me!"

"I'm serious."

"We should talk about this," the Wolf said, looking at Howard Hatchett. "Just let me finish my lunch."

He opened his jaws wide and bit down hard on Hatchett's arm. The man cried out in agony.

"Daphne, it's time to huff and puff," Granny said, stepping aside. Daphne placed the kazoo in her mouth and blew a long note. The wind appeared from nowhere, blasting through the surrounding trees and sending leaves and branches flying in all directions. The Wolf released Hatchett and glared at the little girl.

"That belongs to me!" he growled, and he lunged forward. He was nearly on top of Daphne when Robin's arrow sank into the Wolf's arm. He howled in pain and pulled it out. He continued toward the little girl, but Little John knocked him to his knees with his staff. Puck leaped into the air and landed on the Wolf's shoulders. With his sword, he cracked the beast on the top of his head and then backflipped to safety. The monster bellowed in anger and charged forward, pinning Daphne to the ground. But the little girl kept blowing into the kazoo.

All Sabrina could think to do was jump on the Wolf's back. She punched and kicked with all her strength. She could hear him laughing, maybe at her efforts or maybe at the fear in Daphne's face. He opened his mouth and revealed his horrid fangs—and then the wind finally wrapped around him. It was almost visible, a snakelike creature pulling at the Wolf's body.

The Wolf snarled and struggled as if caught in a hunter's trap. He cursed Daphne, bellowed threats, swore he'd tear her limb from limb, but the wind prevented him from harming her. Sabrina, too, was helpless in wind's power. She let go of the Wolf, but the magic was firmly locked around her.

A writhing shadow creature came loose from the Wolf. Like the one that had released Red Riding Hood, it was horrible and unnatural. It snapped and growled like a real animal, with foam dripping from its fearsome jaws. It hovered above them, howling and screaming, helpless in the magic of the wind. Sabrina turned to see the Wolf's reaction, only to find that he was gone. Lying on the ground beneath her was Mr. Canis, unconscious but breathing. She knelt down and took his hand.

"I'm sorry, Mr. Canis. I'm so sorry!" she shouted over the howling wind. There was a horrible noise, like an agonizing whimper, and then the wind disappeared and all was calm.

"Where did it go?" Sabrina asked as she searched for the shadowy madness. Her voice sounded odd, deep and scratchy, but the rest of her body felt wonderful—strong and fast and powerful. Sabrina felt confident and fearless. In fact, she was eager for a confrontation.

She wanted to share the feeling with her sister, but words were hard to find. Her thoughts were cloudy and confusing. She tried to speak, but it came out sounding like a horrible laugh. She turned to Daphne, hoping she might have an explanation, but the little girl was undergoing some kind of transformation. A swirling black fog circled her body, blocking out most of her face. All Sabrina could see were Daphne's eyes. They glowed like two brilliant suns.

"Sabrina, you have to stop this!" Granny cried.

Sabrina was confused. What did the old woman mean? She wasn't doing anything wrong.

"Sabrina, please! Don't make me do this to you," Daphne begged.

"What are you talking about?" Sabrina asked, noticing the shiny toy in her sister's hand.

"You have to fight this!" Daphne said. "I know you're still in there. Don't let him control you!"

"Have you lost your mind? Why are you talking to me like this?" Sabrina asked. When no one replied, she realized her words were only echoing in her own head.

"Fight him, child," a voice said from below, and Sabrina looked down. Mr. Canis lay at her feet—his body, old and withered, pinned down by a huge, fur-covered paw. It was squeezing the life from the old man's chest. She cried out, hoping someone would help her save him, but her cries ceased when she realized the claws that were killing Mr. Canis belonged to her.

I'm the Big Bad Wolf.

Sabrina leaped to her feet and found a dingy mirror on the wall of the ancient house. It confirmed her fears. Her whole body had transformed. Her long blond hair was gone, replaced by thick, matted fur that covered every inch of her face. Her hands were huge, and her fingers curled into vicious claws. She spun around and found a bushy tail. How could this have happened? She roared in fury and smashed the mirror in front of her.

"I'll fix this," someone said from behind her. Sabrina turned to look at the little girl, unsure of who she was or what she wanted. She imagined grabbing the girl and—no—she knew she had to fight the impulse, but how could she? She was so hungry.

"No, Sabrina! Stop!"

And then the wind returned, and everything went black.

When she woke, Sabrina found herself in a bed in the wooden house that Red Riding Hood's grandmother had slept in hundreds of years before. Her family was standing around her. Daphne was crying and wiping the tears on her sleeve. Uncle Jake was pacing nervously. Granny was holding her hand. Mr. Canis was there, too, holding a glass jar. Inside it, Sabrina could see a dark, black creature zipping back and forth, desperate to escape. Briar, her fairy godmothers, Snow, and Charming were there, as well as Robin, Little John, and the rest of the merry men.

"How are you feeling, child?" Canis asked.

"Normal," Sabrina replied, checking her arms to make sure they were free of fur.

Canis chuckled. "It's a wonderful feeling."

"Is it over?" she asked him.

He nodded. "In a manner of speaking."

Granny Relda bent down and felt her forehead. "You've had quite a day," the old woman said as sirens approached.

"Here comes Nottingham," Robin said. "So, are we decided?"

"Decided?" Sabrina asked.

Charming and Canis looked each other in the eye and shook hands. "Yes, I believe we are," Canis said.

"What's going on?" Sabrina asked.

"I'm afraid that—after you and your family—the rest of us have become Ferryport Landing's most wanted," Charming explained.

"Right where we belong," Little John added cheerfully.

Canis smiled slightly. "It appears that it is in all our best interests to join forces."

"To fight back against the Master and his Scarlet Hand," Robin said.

"We're going into the mountains where no one will find us," Snow explained. "And we're preparing for war."

"You're going, too?" Sabrina asked the teacher.

Snow nodded, then turned to Charming. "Someone has to look after this bunch of troublemakers."

"We'll miss you, old friend," Granny said to Canis.

"I won't be far," the old man promised, then turned to Puck. "You're in charge, boy."

"Haven't I always been?" Puck said with a grin.

One of the merry men raced into the room. "They're coming down the path."

"Then we're off," Robin said. "Don't worry, people. You're going to like the forest."

The group hurried out of the room. Canis turned back for one last moment. "They say my name was Tobias Clay?"

Sabrina nodded.

"I'm very eager to get to know him." A moment later he was gone.

Nottingham dragged the family to the jailhouse for questioning, but after several hours he released them. Despite his anger, he had no proof that anyone in the Grimm family was responsible for freeing the Wolf, killing Bluebeard, or inciting the riot. Still, he made it clear that he would soon have all of them at the ends of nooses, even the children.

Uncle Jake dropped Briar Rose at her coffee shop and promised to call later. She smiled and whispered something in his ear. He grinned like a child on Christmas morning and watched her walk away.

"What did she say?" Daphne asked.

"She said she is in love with me."

"Barf!" Puck gagged.

When they got home, Sabrina was startled to see Nurse Sprat waiting for them on the front porch.

"Nurse Sprat," Granny called when she got out of the car. "We're very sorry we're late. We were detained by the sheriff."

"No problem, Mrs. Grimm. I hope you aren't in any trouble."

"Trouble is practically our middle name," Granny said.

"I brought the girl. She's around here somewhere—oh, here she comes," Sprat said. Sabrina was shocked when Red Riding Hood bounded around the corner with Elvis in tow.

"Is this your doggy?" Red asked. "He's so much fun."

Elvis licked the girl happily.

"What is she doing here?" Sabrina asked.

Granny knelt down to eye level with Red. "She's coming to live with us."

"What?"

"Mr. Canis asked us to look after her while he's away, and I think it's a wonderful idea. Red needs some friends while she adjusts."

Red kissed Elvis on the snout and giggled.

"But she tried to kill us," Sabrina said.

"Sabrina, don't hold a grudge. If I turned away everyone in this town who's tried to kill me, I wouldn't have any friends at all."

Granny set Red up in Mr. Canis's old bedroom and promised she would take the child shopping the next day for some more modern clothing. Sabrina followed her sister upstairs, tired as a dog but eager to plan for what they should do if Red became dangerous again. But Daphne went to Granny's room, as promised, closing the door in Sabrina's face.

Sabrina went to bed alone, but without Daphne the room seemed too big. She tossed and turned, and though she was exhausted, she couldn't sleep. After a while, she decided to visit her parents. She crawled in bed between them and closed her eyes, and she was almost asleep when she heard Mirror clear his throat.

"Want to see where Goldilocks is?" he asked when his face appeared in the reflection.

Sabrina fought back tears. "She doesn't want to come back. Not that I can blame her, really. If I could get out of this town, I would never come back."

"I know exactly how you feel," Mirror said.

Sabrina watched his face disappear. She reached over and kissed her father on the cheek, then her mother. Her kisses weren't magical. They wouldn't wake Henry and Veronica. But maybe they made a difference to her parents. They certainly made a difference to her. She closed her eyes and drifted off to sleep.

Sometime in the night, she heard a knock on the front door. She went downstairs, wondering who could be visiting at such a late hour. Maybe it was just Puck. He was always forgetting his keys. Or maybe Red had decided to have a look around and locked herself out. But when she opened the door, she found someone unexpected waiting.

Three enormous brown bears were on the porch: one in a hat and tie, a second in a purple polka-dotted dress, and the third in a New York Yankees baseball cap. Two of the bears stood nearly eight feet tall, but the smallest was just a few inches taller than Sabrina. A fourth individual pushed her way to the front of the pack. She had big green eyes, tight blond curls, and freckles.

"Goldilocks?" Sabrina gasped.

The woman nodded. "Sorry I'm late. I had to pick up a few friends." Goldilocks smiled. "So, I hear someone in this house needs a kiss."

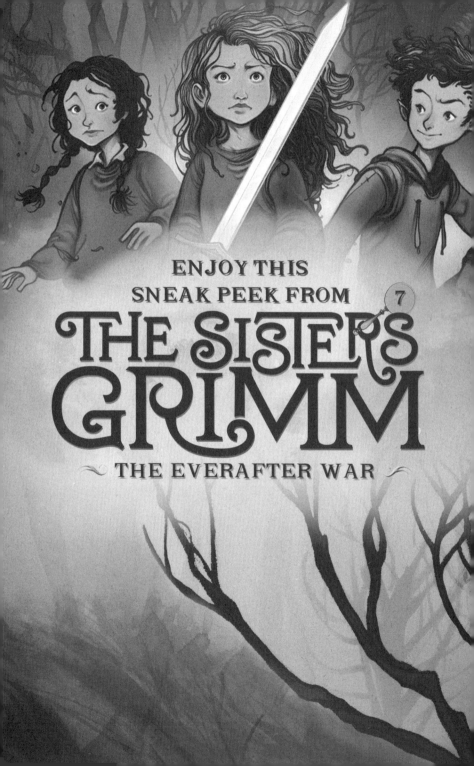

1

SABRINA GRIMM'S LIFE WAS A COLLECTION OF peculiar, almost unbelievable events. But sitting in her grandmother's living room with three massive brown bears had to be the most peculiar of all.

The bears in question arrived with a blond, curly-haired woman. She was a beauty, with a big smile, dimples in both cheeks, and a dainty nose sprinkled with freckles. Her name was Goldilocks. Yes, *the* Goldilocks, but all grown-up and overflowing with nervous energy.

She kept rushing around the living room rearranging things. She moved lamps and rugs, switched furniture around, and even rehung family portraits on different walls. When she moved something, she would step back to study it, mutter something incomprehensible to herself, and then move it again. Once she finally liked where it landed, she would beam with pride and say, "Just right."

Sabrina watched Goldilocks from a love seat across the room. Her little sister, Daphne, sat next to her. At their feet sat the Grimm family's two-hundred-pound Great Dane, Elvis. He turned his big head back and forth from Sabrina and Daphne to the bears and Goldilocks. Every few seconds he let out a soft, confused whine. Sabrina understood how he felt.

"Just another day in Ferryport Landing, Elvis," she said to the dog, and then turned to her sister. "How long are we going to wait?"

Daphne shrugged. "Granny said she'd come and get us as soon as she could. Maybe we should offer them something to eat, to be polite."

"Like what? A trout?"

Goldilocks grunted and huffed and the bears responded with a series of short grunts. They seemed to be talking with one another, but Sabrina couldn't understand any of it. When they finished up their odd chat, Goldilocks told Sabrina that the biggest of the bears would love a cup of Earl Grey tea, very hot. The second biggest would prefer iced tea. The littlest of the bears would like some chocolate milk, if it wasn't too much trouble.

"We'll be right back," Daphne promised, pulling her sister into the kitchen with Elvis in tow. There, they found a little girl in red pajamas huddled in a corner.

"Are they gone yet?" Red Riding Hood whispered.

"No," Daphne said. "But they're friends, Red. You don't have to hide."

Red didn't look convinced. She tried to squeeze deeper into the corner.

Daphne went to work preparing the drinks while Sabrina spied on their guests through the crack in the kitchen door. "Goldilocks is giving me a headache," Sabrina admitted. "Why can't she sit still?"

"Don't spy," Daphne scolded. "It's rude."

"Aren't you curious about her? Dad was in love with her before he met Mom." Sabrina studied the woman. Goldilocks was very pretty, and she seemed nice enough. But she was no Veronica Grimm. Sabrina's mom was a knockout.

"Love is weird," Daphne said with a hint of authority.

Sabrina laughed. "And you're an expert? You're only—" She stopped herself when she spotted her sister's scowl. Sabrina was already treading on thin ice with Daphne. "Yeah, you're right. Love is weird."

"Red, won't you please join us?" Daphne asked kindly when the drinks were ready.

Red shook her head vigorously, staring down at the floor.

The sisters carried the tray of drinks into the living room.

"This is a bad idea," Goldilocks fretted. She sat on the ottoman, only to jump up again, rush across the room, and move a vase an inch to the left. "I shouldn't have come here. Your father is not going to be happy."

"He'll understand. We've tried everything we can think of to wake them up. You're our last hope," Sabrina said, nearly panicked that the woman might change her mind.

"I tried to respect his wishes. I moved to New York City and lived there for a long time. I had a nice little apartment in the East Village. Even when I heard he and Veronica had moved to Manhattan, I never went to see him. I avoided the fairy kingdom in Central Park in case he ever went there. It was my way of showing that I was sorry for what happened to his dad, and now, here I am, breaking my promise to stay out of his life. When he opens his eyes and sees me standing over him, he's going to be furious. And your mother! She's going to think I'm a . . . a harlot!"

"What's *harlot* mean?" Daphne asked.

"A harlot is—" Sabrina started.

"I asked Goldilocks, not you," Daphne snapped.

Sabrina's face flushed at the sharp tone. It stung that Daphne wanted as little to do with her as possible

"A harlot is a woman with a bad reputation. A harlot is a woman who kisses another woman's husband," Goldilocks explained, and then sighed deeply. "What is keeping your grandmother?"

"Same old Goldie," a voice sang from across the room. Sabrina turned to find Uncle Jake wearing a huge smile. "Just as impatient as I remember. You should see her in a drive-thru restaurant, girls. Fast food isn't fast enough for her."

Goldilocks frowned and moved a paperweight from the coffee

table to the bureau. "Jake Grimm! Don't tease me. I'm a nervous wreck."

"Then let's get this show on the road," he said, gesturing toward the stairs. "We're all ready."

Goldilocks bit her lower lip and, along with the bears, Sabrina, and Daphne, followed Jake.

Granny Relda was waiting at the top of the stairs. She grinned and embraced Goldilocks as if she were one of her own children.

"It's good to see you, Goldie," she said warmly.

Goldilocks smiled and nearly cried at the same time. "It's been a long time, Mrs. Grimm."

"Who is Mrs. Grimm? Call me Relda, honey," she said, then turned to Sabrina. "Where is our friend Red?"

"Being weird in the kitchen."

"Red!" the old woman called out, and a few moments later the little girl appeared at the bottom of the steps.

"Are you coming?" the old woman asked.

Red shook her head. "This is your family. I don't belong."

Granny gestured for her to join them. "Come along, *liebling*."

Reluctantly, Red climbed the stairs, and Granny led everyone into a spare bedroom furnished with a mirror and a queen-size bed. Lying comfortably on the mattress were Sabrina and Daphne's parents, Henry and Veronica Grimm. Both were in a deep, enchanted sleep.

Goldie looked like she was about to faint. She leaned against the bedroom wall to keep upright. "Relda, I—"

Granny Relda waved her off. "There's nothing to apologize for. What happened to Basil was not your fault. It wasn't anyone's fault."

Sabrina watched Uncle Jake study the floor. She wondered if he would ever forgive himself for his part in Basil's death.

"I appreciate your kindness but I'm not sure Henry feels the same way," Goldie said. "How long have they been like this?"

"They were kidnapped two years ago," Daphne explained. "We only got them back a few months ago. So far as we know, they've been like this the whole time."

"Did you try Prince Charming?" Goldilocks said. "He has a knack for waking up people with a kiss."

"The women he wakes up tend to fall in love with him," Granny said. "It might be coincidence, but we'd rather not chance it."

"We don't want William Charming for a stepfather," Sabrina grumbled.

Uncle Jake crossed the room to Poppa Bear and patted his furry arm affectionately. "Good to see you again, old man. Your boy is getting big."

"You know the bears?" Goldilocks asked.

Uncle Jake nodded. "Oh yes. Let's just say Poppa and Baby helped me retrieve a phantom scroll from a Romanian constable a few years back."

"Retrieve or steal, Jacob?" Goldilocks asked, raising her eyebrows.

Momma Bear growled. Sabrina didn't need to speak bear to hear her disapproval.

"I don't mean to be rude," Sabrina interrupted. "But we've been waiting a long time for this to happen. Could we all catch up after we wake up Mom and Dad?"

"Of course," Goldilocks said. "So, Jake, you're the expert on magic. Do I just kiss Henry and he'll wake up?"

"That's the word on the street," Uncle Jake said. "Briar Rose was under a similar spell and she says there's no special trick to it. Just pucker up and lay one on him."

"Briar Rose said 'pucker up and lay one on him'?" Goldilocks asked.

"I'm paraphrasing," Uncle Jake said.

"This all depends on whether you still love my son," Granny said.

Goldie looked down at Henry and gave his hand a squeeze. "What about Veronica? I'm not going to be any help to her."

"Dad will take over once he's awake," Daphne reassured her.

"OK, here goes," Goldilocks said. She tucked a curl behind her ear and leaned in close to Henry. She hovered, her face just inches from his, and whispered something Sabrina couldn't hear. Then, she pressed her lips to his and closed her eyes.

ABOUT THE AUTHOR

Michael Buckley is the *New York Times*–bestselling author of the Sisters Grimm and NERDS series, *Kel Gilligan's Daredevil Stunt Show*, and the Undertow Trilogy. He has also written and developed television shows for many networks. Michael lives in Brooklyn, New York, with his wife, Alison; their son, Finn; and their dog, Friday.